S0-ARN-196

$2

The Snake on the Grave

ALSO BY GEORGE BEARE

The Bloody Sun at Noon
The Very Breath of Hell
The Bee Sting Deal

The
Snake
on the
Grave

GEORGE BEARE

**MIDNIGHT
NOVEL OF
SUSPENSE**

HOUGHTON MIFFLIN COMPANY BOSTON 1974

FIRST PRINTING   C

FIRST AMERICAN EDITION 1974

Copyright © 1973 by George Beare
All rights reserved. No part of this work may be reproduced
or transmitted in any form by any means, electronic or
mechanical, including photocopying and recording, or by
any information storage or retrieval system, without
permission in writing from the publisher.

Library of Congress Cataloging in Publication Data

Beare, George
    The snake on the grave.

    (Midnight novel of suspense)
    I. Title.
PZ4.B3687Sn3   [PR6052.E19]   823/.9/14   73–19795
ISBN 0–395–18468–1

PRINTED IN THE UNITED STATES OF AMERICA

The Snake on the Grave

1

Jack Carmody had been sent down for twenty years, which is a long sentence when you consider that all he did was steal two pictures, even though the pictures were probably worth two or three million pounds. There was a reason, however, for the severity—the pictures had not been recovered, and Carmody refused to say what he had done with them. It is widely known that the law does not do deals with criminals, but it was a fair bet that if they had got those pictures back Carmody would have been out in five.

He was fifty-four when he went down, and to a man of fifty-four, twenty years is as good as life; but it did not shake him, and he still refused to talk. Then somebody else tried a different tack. More people than just the law and the insurance company were looking for those pictures, and these other people were not subject to the same restrictions as the official investigators. They could play dirty.

Shortly after his committal to Parkhurst Prison, Jack Carmody received a message from persons unknown that told him in effect that if he did not divulge the whereabouts of the pictures, his wife and daughter were going to be hit. Jack Carmody decided then that there was only one man in the world who could help him, an old friend named Latch.

At this time, Black and White Sammy Latch was playing a club in Newcastle upon Tyne. He was also playing a bit of cards and a horse or two; but his main occupation was the piano—the gambling was just for money. He was living in a flat at Whitley Bay, driving a fire-engine-red E-type Jaguar, and in bed working his way through the kids in the chorus line at the club just to keep his eye in in that department; it was not a particularly satisfying or fulfilling way of life, but one to which, through necessity and inertia, he had become accustomed. He had been clean now for several years —they had even let him have his passport back so that he could go on tour in the course of his work, and he was so respectable and accepted a member of the musical profession that his hands were insured for a hundred thousand pounds with Lloyd's of London. The only times the law bothered him now were when he neglected his alimony payments or the irritating demands of the Inland Revenue. Now, it seemed, Big Jack was in trouble, and because Big Jack had been a friend for many years, among other reasons, Latch felt it incumbent upon him to help in any way he could.

Thus, one morning, he flew down to London to talk to this lawyer, Wallace, whose offices were in St. Martin's Lane.

'How are you fixed, Sammy?' the lawyer asked him.

'I'm all right,' Latch said, and shrugged.

Wallace said, 'Somebody got a message through to Big Jack in Parkhurst to this effect: Unless he discloses the exact whereabouts of the canvasses, Big Jack's wife and daughter are going to be hit.'

'Does he know who it is?'

Wallace passed a piece of paper across his desk. It was a strip torn off a roll of Government-issue toilet paper and written on with a ball-point pen. 'A fellow who got out of Parkhurst on Saturday night brought it to me yesterday,' the lawyer said. 'That's when I phoned you.'

Latch read the letter; it said:

'Dear Lee: It is possible you will get a number of letters like this because there are three or four people getting out over the next week or so and I'm sending one with each of them in case a couple forget to deliver or get stopped or something. I just hope to God one of them gets through. Somebody knows where Marcia and Rachel are. I've got to spill about where the pictures are by the end of this month or they are going to hit my wife and daughter. The kid first, then if I still don't spill, Marci. It could be a con, but I'm not about to bet on that as the sod who delivered this message to me is in for gbh and I know for a fact that he has worked for Franco Porcia. I want you to get hold of Sammy Latch, you know Black and White Sammy who used to play piano at the Sundowner. He knows how to use himself and he's a good friend and he used to be sweet on Marci before she married me—if he still feels just a little bit that way about her, he'll help out now, I'm sure. Find him and tell him the score. What he is going to have to do is get Marcia and Rachel away to the States or Canada or somewhere, even South America if he can, before the end of the month, when I think there'll be a contract out for one or both of them in Europe, Sammy will know how to handle it. I can't spill about the pictures, Lee, because there are more people than me involved in that deal, so for Christ's sake get Sammy working on it fast as you can.'

7

The letter was signed 'John Carmody', which is how Big Jack referred to himself, always formally. Latch handed the letter back to the lawyer. It was genuine. Then he stood up and started pacing, thinking.

'What are you thinking about?' Wallace asked him.

'Porcia,' he said. 'Porcia is the Organisation, mate. The Mafia. Where can I take them where the Mafia won't find them?'

Wallace shrugged. 'Big Jack is of the opinion that you will be able to work that one out for yourself.'

'If it came to the crunch,' Latch asked, 'I mean to save his kid's and his wife's lives, would he spill about the pictures?'

'Sammy,' the lawyer said, 'you know him probably better than I do.'

Latch nodded. 'Where are they then?' he asked.

'In the south of France. A place called La Ciotat.'

For a while Latch continued pacing deep in thought. Then he said, 'I'll have to go back to Newcastle to pick up my passport and my car. It'll mean bucking my contract with Romano's up there. Do you think you could square that for me?'

'Leave it to me,' the lawyer said.

2

Flying north that evening, Black and White Sammy Latch considered the backside of the stewardess as she leaned over a passenger across the aisle from him. As an arse it was not one of the all-time greats, but it would probably get her whatever she needed if she used it wisely. The No Smoking sign had gone out so he lit one and waited for the other stewardess to bring the drink he had ordered before take-off. He thought about Jack Carmody and Marcia; particularly he thought about Marcia. There was an arse that was more than an all-time great; Marcia Carmody's derrière was a classic, as were her breasts and her legs and her entire damn system. She sang with a voice clean and free as a bird soaring in a still, blue sky, and she had hair like black silk and eyes like pools of wet tar.

Jack used to own the Sundowner Club in Curzon Street, before the rackets ruined him, and Latch had played the piano there and Marcia sang. Records she made then were still selling, and sometimes, if he was driving out to the races or somewhere and he just idly flicked on the car radio, they might be playing one of them, usually it was 'Fly Me To The Moon', and it was just like six inches of cold steel in the guts for Latch, and he would have to switch it off quick.

Jack Carmody had flown Spitfires in the Battle of

Britain, one of the Few, a man who had been to hell and survived to come back with medals and glory all over him.

Sammy Latch had been seven years old when the war started and when the Blitz on London came he had been evacuated down to Somerset, thus avoiding the bomb that had levelled his home in the Mile End Road and killed his mother, his older brother and sister, and an aunt. One of Rommel's .88's had taken care of his old man somewhere in the Western Desert, and that had left Latch all on his lonesome. He had learned to play the piano on that farm down in Somerset because it was the only thing that dulled the pain in him of knowing that he was never going to see his mother or father or his brother or sister ever again. The piano then became the only other member of the Latch family. From time to time he still went back there to the farm to visit the old couple who had looked after him then; they were very old now, but always glad to have him whenever he turned up.

After the war he went fighting. He had never really known why, it was just a thing he had wanted to do, and Jack Carmody had picked him up as a sixteen-year-old, long, gangling, hard-eyed kid in Brendan O'Connor's gym down in Lizard Street, Stepney, in 1948, and subsequently signed him as a pro in '52, after Latch had done two years in the army. Latch had fought at welterweight and at that time was only ever beaten on disqualifications, the Board of Control finally revoking his permit for persistent failure to abide by the Marquess of Queensberry. It did not bother Latch much, it was just a thing he had wanted to do and now had done and got off his chest, so he took the ban philosophically and went back to learning the piano. That is what he had really wanted to do all along, anyway, and eventually he was good enough to take it up full-time, even though it did not pay very well.

The ban, however, at the time meant economic disaster. All the loot Jack Carmody got on his discharge from the R.A.F. had been spent on fighters, none of whom had shown the potential Latch had, and so in effect when Latch was tossed out, so was Jack, and they had found themselves in the gutter together. To pay for piano lessons, food, and somewhere to sleep, in that order of priority, Latch joined Big Jack conning, dud cheques, stealing cars, milking petrol from the American bases, little rackets with ration books and nylon stockings and stuff like that. They were caught and sent down for six months. When they came out, Latch returned to the piano and Big Jack worked at a number of enterprises, mostly illegal, like organising card games in hotel rooms, and probably running a whore-stable as well, but Latch had never delved too deeply into it. Then one night he came and informed Latch that he had bought himself the lease on a night-club and he wanted Latch to come and play the piano there, and it was about then that Marcia arrived on the scene as well.

When Marcia married Big Jack, Latch left the club and went conning again, and got caught again and sent down again, and inside he took up the noble art again. The first time he had gone fighting was just after the war in which he lost his family; the second time was just after another kind of war, in which he had lost Marcia. It just came on him again, the urge to fight. But this time, tougher and far more mature than the other, he made more of a go of it. When he came out of jail the Board of Control, under a little pressure from

11

the prison authorities, was persuaded to lift the ban on him and he went on to hold a British and Commonwealth title. The money came in easier and he learned to live well and got married and had a home for the first time since he was seven years old; but it had not worked out for him, and it had all come down around his ears the night he was floored in the eighth round in a fight at Madison Square Garden. He had debts he couldn't pay and a wife who didn't want to know him. He went back to the piano and of the little he made out of that, the Inland Revenue took most of it and the ex-wife took the remainder.

Big Jack Carmody had bailed him out, paid his tax debt and took him on back at the Sundowner, where he played again for Marcia and where they used to say that she never sang sweeter than when Black and White Sammy was accompanying her. She was big-time now, getting to be heard abroad and when the Sands in Vegas offered her a stand she took Latch with her to play for her there, and some of the light that shone on her inevitably began to bathe Latch in its warm and successful glow as well. It was there that Marcia first realised how much she had hurt Latch by marrying Jack Carmody, and it was in Vegas that she had first slept with Latch. The affair continued whenever they were working out of England and it went on for several years, until the Sundowner folded up; the protection boys had moved in and Big Jack had refused to pay. The law started hearing about the drinks he served after hours and the big stud games in the back room; staff became difficult to recruit and once recruited didn't last long; drunks began making scenes in the club room; the place started to run down and Carmody was losing money. If it hadn't been for that, Marcia would have left him then and cloven to Latch. But Big Jack was in trouble and she refused to quit him while he needed her, so she began subsidising him and went on subsidising him until they were both broke and he had to close the place and live on her income.

She stopped taking up offers from abroad and they moved into a house at Wimbledon. Latch was all right now, mainly through his association with Marcia; he was doing a lot of television and playing in places like the Festival and the Royal Albert Halls. Also he cut a few LPs of his own, that sold well, so he was riding along getting good offers and plenty of them.

Life for Big Jack, though, had become hell. He despised himself for living on Marcia's income, but could find no acceptable alternative. He began hatching plots, shady real estate and stocks and shares deals, some of which made him a quid or two, but nothing spectacular, until he met this character he had known somewhere during the war, and out of this meeting had come the tip that had led to the big one, the pictures job.

The pictures were a Goya and an old master. For some reason they were being flown from Amsterdam to London, and somehow Big Jack had managed to intercept them. He had had a plane waiting for him at an airport out in Essex, a hired job that he piloted himself, because he could still fly a plane, old Jack, and less than two hours after the robbery he was in that plane and heading east. Twenty-four hours later he was back, without the pictures, and the police were there waiting for him when he landed. Where he'd been was the big mystery, but they reckoned he'd had time to get to Germany and back.

The pictures were hidden, and as Latch reasoned it

13

now they were going to remain hidden. Even with full remission for good conduct and all the rest, Big Jack was not going to be out of Parkhurst much before he was seventy. Big Jack, it seemed, was finished. Certainly he was finished unless he could do a deal over those pictures. They were his one last ace in the hole.

3

A man like Franco Porcia is a big crocodile in his own little neck of the swamp, but in the overall picture of the swamp hierarchy he is not so big, he is only a fang of a far bigger crocodile that is the Organisation. There would be another fang in the south of France, in Marseilles or Toulon, who would be handling that end of the operation and it occurred to Latch to wonder whether it was worthwhile trying to find out the name and address of the man in charge of the Organisation's Côte d'Azur chapter. He could probably have found out—by spending some money and asking some questions of a few people in town, he could have known before he even left for France exactly who was observing Marcia and Rachel in La Ciotat. He decided against it, for one reason because he did not want to telegraph the information that he was dealing himself into the game, and for another, having given it some thought, he did not believe that Porcia, or any other Organisation agent, was the man he needed really to concern himself with.

That man was the prime mover and it wasn't Porcia or any other member of the brotherhood because they do not concern themselves with larceny, however grand. No one in the Organisation would touch a hot

Goya with a twenty-foot cucumber. Somebody, somewhere was paying them to put the screws on Jack Carmody, and in all probability not even Porcia himself knew who it was. It could have been somebody in New York working through the East Coast chapter, or somebody in Hong Kong, or Beirut, or anywhere.

The day after the interview with Wallace in London, Latch and his car flew by Channel Air Bridge to Calais, from where Latch drove to Paris and put the car and himself on a train for Marseilles. It was an overnight run and he occupied a sleeper, arriving at the Gare St. Charles at about eight a.m. He booked into an hotel on the Boulevard d'Athenes just down the hill from the station and had a shower and a shave and a change of clothes.

The day was hot and bright with sun. He put the top of the Jag down and drove up from the hotel's basement car park and along into the traffic on the Canebière. At the Rue de Rome he turned left, tooling along in second with the traffic towards the Place Castellane, a tall, lean, pale-skinned man with a hard, tightly-pursed mouth, eyes hidden by wraparound sun glasses, a black mane of hair thinning on top but long over the ears and the sideburns and down the back of the neck. He wore a black, short-sleeve cotton sport shirt and he looked good, which he wasn't, and in the gleaming red E-type he looked moderately rich, which he also wasn't; but as he came up into the steep rise of the Avenue du Prado under the beetling cliffs of granite that wall Marseilles and with the statue of Notre-Dame de la Garde towering above the crudely stacked roofs and gazing out to the Med on his right, women walking on the footpaths turned and watched him pass.

Soon he was burning around the wide white concrete Route Nationale 559 in the direction of Cassis and La Ciotat, which is a sleepy little sunbaked place that used to be a fishing port and is now—like all the sleepy little sunbaked places that used to be fishing ports in the south of France—a tourist trap.

4

Along with all the other tourists he parked his car on the promenade and began an aimless tour of the beach-front bars. It was Sunday and they were crowded and ablaze with juke-box music. He ogled the girls, nearly naked and brown as new-baked biscuits, and drank a few beers. He did not want to ask anyone for directions because it meant giving away certain things, like the fact that he had an interest in the building Marcia Carmody was living in. He would find it on his own.

At length he came to a post office displaying a large plan of the town on a board standing on a patch of sandy lawn in front. He studied the plan for nearly ten minutes before finding the street he needed. It looked like a dead-end and it was right at the back of the town, on the side farthest from the beach, up towards where the hills rose abruptly from the shoreline covered in dry, dusty scrub and pines, dotted by the occasional old stone villa of the better-heeled. Taking his time in the heat he walked up that way on a broad empty street of broken pavé half hidden under shallow sand drifts brought down by the Mistral. He turned a corner and passed through a deserted shopping centre, boxes of fruit leaning under a coloured canvas awning attracting flies, an empty supermarket, a small bar with nobody at either of its sidewalk tables. In the heat of the day everybody was inside.

He walked the length of a broad, sandy, sun-baked

street down which he could have fired a rifle without hazard to a living soul and at the end in the great silence of the heat he turned left into Marcia Carmody's street.

There was no name on it, but the post office map said it was the Rue d'Iena, a somewhat grandiose title for an unpaved gravel dead-end, but the residences off it were not so humble, large houses in plenty of ground shaded by plane trees and eucalypti and tall pines, most with swimming pools. The place Marcia Carmody lived in however was an apartment block of about ten floors, her floor being the sixth. It was the last building in the street and beyond its grounds was scrub and tall, un-tended grass. There were cars parked under the shade of a grove of palms at the edge of the lawn and the con-crete awning cantilevered out from above the front en-trance, but no sign of life. Out in the middle of the lawn a swimming pool lay torpid and unused amid a kaleido-scope of sun-umbrellas shielding deserted chairs and tables. On one or two of the tables stood an empty spa water or Coke bottle, and a few plastic cups.

It had been a long walk in the heat and Latch was feeling a thirst now. He could not hang around here too long, he had just wanted a look at the place, and now that he had seen it he returned down the gravel slope, making for the little bar he had passed on the way up.

When he reached it he found about three customers in it, plus a fat man behind the counter and a skinny, middle-aged woman waiting on the tables. There was the inevitable juke-box, pinball machine and one-armed bandit, and through an open doorway at the back a crowd of men could be seen standing in the dappled shade of a big tree there, playing boule. Latch bought a beer and went out under the tree with them, standing on the fringes of the group, watching the boule game. The clear area they were playing on was bounded by undergrowth and, on one side, a road that would run parallel with the Rue d'Iena. Most of the rich houses of the Rue d'Iena were hidden by trees away on the right, but Latch now observed that from here, above the scrub and through the leaves of high trees to the north, the upper storeys of Marcia Carmody's apartment block could be seen. This meant, he reasoned, that the place could be approached from the rear, and under cover through the bush.

These discoveries decided him on his next move. He went back down to the seafront and behaved like a tourist for the rest of the afternoon and in the early evening had dinner alone at the Rose du Thé, a hotel on the promenade that fed him on fruits de mer, veal escalope and salade Nicoise with a bottle of white Burgundy, and then some camembert with a couple of slugs of Calvados to moisten it. By the time he had eaten, it was dark. He went to his car and took a canvas windcheater from the boot, then he went back up the hill, the way he had gone earlier in the day, but not taking the right turn down to the Rue d'Iena, carrying on straight up past the bar on the corner. The steep gravel road was unlit and he was in darkness. On the other side of the road were some big houses, set well back behind walls and trees. On this side was the overgrown vacant ground. He kept on up until, through the trees, he could see the apartment block again, lights shining in its upper windows, then he quit the road and headed into the scrub. After twenty minutes of picking his way through the long grass and bush he entered a brake of trees on the edge of the lawn surrounding the apartment block. Here he sat down, leaning back against the trunk of a tree.

He counted the floors up to six. There were no lights in Marcia Carmody's place. He waited. Some people emerged from the front of the building and drove off in a car. At about ten o'clock, three people came out and a big car, a Mercedes, that had been one of those parked under the palm trees over by the far lawn, swung round to pick them up; Latch had to move behind the tree to avoid being caught by its headlights as it turned. The people piled in and the Merc moved off down the gravel drive to the Rue d'Iena. There were more comings and goings but no light appeared in the windows on the sixth floor. Then, shortly after 1 a.m., a car came up the drive from the street; from its exhaust noise it was a fast car and it was not dilly-dallying now, it came sideways round the curve of the drive, broadsiding to a halt under the entrance canopy. It was a dark Porsche, maybe black, and its windows were down because when it stopped Latch could hear its occupants talking. They spoke in English, a man and a girl, the girl thoroughly-thoroughly English, the man with a German accent.

'. . . let me come up with you,' the man was saying, 'if she's there I will come down again.'

The girl said, 'You didn't really have to come in at a hundred bloody miles an hour like that. She might have been asleep, but she certainly isn't now.' As she spoke the passenger-side door opened and the girl got out of the car. 'Wait here,' she said. 'I won't take a minute.'

The driver's door opened. 'I know your minutes, *Liebchen*, they can be longer than hours.'

'It only seems like that because we're apart, darling,'

21

the girl said. Latch could see her now in silhouette against the moonlit drive and she was young and very beautiful and had long black hair and wore only a bikini. The car had been blocking Latch's view of the man, but now his silhouette emerged into view as well.

'Come here,' the man said to the girl.

'I thought we were in a hurry,' the girl said, but moved up to him and their silhouettes melded. As the couple embraced, standing there on the drive at the back end of the Porsche, Latch had a disconcerting vision of himself being picked up by the gendarmes for voyeurism. He had another uncomfortable feeling, too, concerning the girl. Could she be Rachel Carmody? The last time Latch saw her, Marcia's daughter had been twelve, and in the five years from twelve, girls' outlines alter drastically. If she was Rachel, who was the buffalo with her?

The girl had gone into the apartment block, leaving the man standing by the back of the car, lighting a cigarette. All he wore was swim-shorts and leather sandals. He was tall, slender, hard-muscled, with a slab-like Easter Island face and curly blond hair.

He looked up now to the sixth floor and presently saw the lights switched on up there. The girl, it seemed, was Rachel. The lights remained on for eight minutes, then went out. The German had sauntered across the lawn into the shade of some trees to relieve himself. He was coming back as the girl came out of the lobby. She still wore only a bikini but she was carrying a large canvas bag from the top of which the heel-ends of a pair of black rubber flippers projected along with the walking-stick-handle shape of the mouthpiece end of a snorkel tube.

'Was she there?' the German asked her.

'No,' the girl said. 'There was a message on the tape. She's at the Norwoods'. I don't know why she doesn't move in with the bloody Norwoods, she seems to live there.'

'Did you leave a message on the tape for her?' the German asked.

The girl giggled, tossing her bag into the back of the Porsche. 'I won't tell you what it was, it would destroy all your fond illusions about me.'

'I have no illusions about you, *Liebchen*,' the German laughed. They climbed into the car and took off back down the drive and out onto the street.

Latch settled back against his tree and smoked a cigarette in the darkness. About an hour later another car came up the drive, a small, white convertible with the top down. It looked like an Alfa. There was a woman driving and she was alone. She parked over by the far lawn and when she got out, from the way she moved, he knew her. She'd cut her hair, but she was Marcia, all her old style still intact, the long-legged flowing walk and the easy grace of a woman who is used to being looked at and knows that the lookers are getting damn good value. She was wearing just a short cotton frock and high-heeled sandals that clop-clopped on the tiles as she came up under the entrance canopy into the light from the lobby and he got a good look at her. Her skin was deeply tanned, a smooth, honey gold, and she'd had her hair cut very short, and dyed. Or maybe, he realised, she was greying, because she was no spring chicken any more, she was pushing forty. But then, the melancholy thought came to him, so are we all. All pushing forty, and come I to drink at Caesar's funeral.

5

After she had gone into the apartment block he sat there in the trees fifteen minutes until he was sure she hadn't been followed. Then he went in after her, across the lobby to the automatic lift, and straight up to the sixth floor. When the lift stopped, Marcia Carmody's voice came to him out of a mesh-covered speaker by his right ear.

'Qui est là?'

Somewhat awkwardly he spoke back at the speaker. 'Marcia,' he said, short of breath, 'it's Sammy. Sammy Latch.'

For a moment the speaker was speechless. Then her voice came from it again, strained and incredulous: 'Sammy?'

'Black and White Sammy,' he said. 'Jack sent me.'

The lift doors slid apart and she was standing about ten feet in front of him with a small, chrome-plated .25 Beretta aimed at his throat; but she only aimed it long enough to ascertain that he was who he claimed to be, and that he was alone. Then she forgot it in the shock of seeing him.

'What in God's name are you doing here?' she whispered.

'Hoping I'll get offered a drink,' he said.

She ran to him and flung her arms round his neck. 'Sammy,' she whimpered, and tears were coming out of her eyes.

They stood there for a long time kissing and just holding on tight. 'I can't believe it,' she kept saying, 'I just can't believe it,' and then she would move her face back to look at him again, and then she would kiss him again, saying, 'Sammy,' again and again, and his face was wet from her tears.

'I've been sitting out in the bloody trees all night,' he told her, 'waiting for you to come home.'

'Why? Why have you been sitting out in the trees?'

Her hair was not greying, it had indeed been dyed, with a nice dark sheen to it like old pewter.

'Come in,' she said, moving back from him and taking him into the living room, wiping her eyes on the back of her hand. 'Why have you been sitting out in the trees all night?'

'Didn't want anybody to see me coming in,' he said.

'You romantic fool, but there was really no necessity for that, the neighbours are quite broad-minded down here. Sit down. What'll you have? Scotch?'

He nodded. 'It wasn't your reputation I was trying to protect,' he said.

'What do you mean? It was your reputation?'

He laughed. Then he said, 'Do you have any kind of a cover here, like an alias? Or does everybody know you're Marcia Carmody?'

'Everybody knows I'm Marcia Carmody. Why, for God's sake, shouldn't everybody? Anyway, what would be the point of an alias? My physog has been on television all over the Western hemisphere, it's on record jackets in every bourgeois living-room between here and the Khyber Pass . . .' she brought two drinks over

25

and put them on the coffee table in front of him, then said, 'Listen, sweetheart, just let me go and straighten my face, will you?'

She hadn't taken in a single word he'd said. He reached out and took her hand. 'Come here,' he said.

'Darling,' she said, 'it's wonderful to see you. I can't tell you how wonderful.'

He leaned down and picked up his drink and swallowed about half of it in one. She realised then that he had something on his mind, other than the usual.

'What is it, Sammy?' she asked. 'Why are you here?'

'Jack got a message in Parkhurst. Either he tells where he's hidden the pictures, or you and Rachel are going to get hit.'

She looked at him blankly. Then she said, 'Hit?'

He nodded, taking another mouthful of Scotch.

'What does hit mean?'

'It means you're going to get a bullet in the back of the head.'

Understandably, she found that difficult to digest; he left her working on it and went to help himself to another drink.

At length she said, 'It's a bluff.'

'No, it isn't.'

'How do you know?'

'Because whether it's a bluff or not, you can't afford to treat it as a bluff. Do you see?'

'Where did this message come from, that Jack received?'

'He's not sure, but he thinks from Franco Porcia.'

'That bastard!'

Porcia was one of the causes of the ruin of Jack Carmody's old enterprise, the Sundowner Club.

26

'If it did come from Porcia,' Latch said, 'he's just an agent, a messenger-boy, hit-man.'

'Then who is he representing?'

'Anyone,' Latch said morosely. 'From what you've told me—that you have no cover and everybody in town knows who you are, it could literally be anyone, barring a few obvious exceptions like maybe the Pope and Mahatma Gandhi.'

'But it could still be a bluff.'

'Are you prepared to chance it? And wake up one morning and find Rachel dead?'

'Then why doesn't he tell them where his bloody pictures are?'

Latch just shrugged.

'I suppose his stinking pictures are more important than his daughter's life!' she continued.

'I don't think so, Marci,' Latch said softly, and inadequately.

'Fix me a drink, Sammy,' she said. 'Please.'

He took her empty glass from her and went back to the liquor cabinet. While he was fixing the drink he said to her: 'Look, some anonymous bastard has barked at Jack. You can't expect him to lie down and shake all over because some anonymous bastard has barked at him.'

'And what are you going to do?' she asked.

He brought the drink to her, keeping away from the windows when he moved. 'We've got a little time. Till the end of the month, ten days. Jack wanted me to get you and Rachel away somewhere. South America, maybe.'

'Great,' she said. 'Just bloody-well fantastic. We hop to South America. Until somebody there recognises me. Then we hop to North America, then we hop to

27

bloody Tibet, and then I spend the rest of my life hopping around the bloody universe like the wandering kangaroo, keeping one hop ahead of a bullet in the back of the skull, just to keep his rotten pictures safe for him. No, I won't, Sammy. I've done enough for Jack. I've sacrificed my career for him. I wouldn't have minded that if he'd appreciated it, but he didn't and he still doesn't. Now I'm finished with the sod and you can go back to him, Sammy, and tell him the ball is back in his court, because I'm not shifting and neither is Rachel. Bluff or no, we're staying put right here and he can tell them where the pictures are or watch his daughter and his wife get hit, as you put it, whichever he prefers.'

She was right, of course. Old Jack had not really thought the thing through very succinctly. But the idea had occurred to Latch in the lawyer's office in London. What really was the point in getting her out? Porcia's outfit had feelers everywhere. Wherever he took Marcia and Rachel, sooner or later one of those feelers would locate them.

Or maybe Jack had thought it out.

And if the lawyer had put to Latch what Jack really wanted him to do, Latch would not have taken the commission gold-plated. What Big Jack Carmody really wanted Latch to do, all that Latch really could do now, was find the prime mover.

6

It was 4 a.m., about two hours to dawn.

'Where's Rachel now?' he asked her.

'With Klaus von Schanze.'

'Is he a tall young Kraut who drives a black Porsche?'

She looked up at him. 'Yes. That's Klaus. How did you know?'

'They came in while I was sitting out in the trees. Rachel came upstairs and packed a bag, then they took off again. About an hour before you came in.'

'The little bitch,' Marcia said with feeling.

'What did you say?' Latch asked, mildly surprised.

'I've asked her, begged her, to keep away from this fellow. We've had frightful rows over him, but it has no effect.'

'Why do you object to him?'

'He's married, for one thing,' she said. Then she added, glancing at him, 'Oh, I know I'm the last one on earth who should preach about that; but they're —they're an unsavoury lot—the von Schanzes and the crowd they associate with. Idle, corrupt rich. Von Schanze's wife doesn't seem to mind about his association with Rachel, in fact it appears to amuse her. She's an American named Raejean, a real brass-bound bitch.'

'And you can't stop Rachel seeing this fellow?'

'Not without locking her in the loo and standing guard twenty-four hours a day.'

'This Klaus,' Latch asked, 'I suppose he knows who you are and why you're living here?'

'I suppose he does.'

'Who else knows, that you can name?'

She shrugged. 'The Norwoods. Lord and Lady Norwood, you know them, they're old friends, they used to come to the Sundowner a lot. He was a mad gambler. Still is.'

Latch nodded. He remembered them vaguely from the big card games in the back rooms at the Sundowner. 'What are they doing down here?'

'They've been living down here for about two years now. They have a villa down near Bandol.'

'Do you have any boy friends?' he asked her.

She laughed. 'Hundreds, darling,' she said.

Then he asked, 'Why do you carry a gun, Marcia?'

'Protection,' she said. 'You know how it is in this business. A girl is the object of all sorts of attentions from all sorts of admirers, some of whom are not very welcome and need to be convinced of the fact. There was a scene one night at a place called l'Hirondelle, which is a casino at Cap Benat. This fellow followed me home here and got in and I had to start screaming and the police were involved and it was all very distasteful, and after that Freddie Norwood got me the gun. I've never fired it, I doubt if I'd be able to hit anything if I did fire it, but it's a comfort.'

'Tell me something,' he said to her. 'The truth.'

'What?'

'Do you know where the pictures are?'

His eyes held hers for a moment, and she hesitated

30

just a moment too long, before she looked away. 'No,' she said.

He remembered what Jack had said in the letter to the lawyer in London, about his being unable to say where the pictures were because there were more people than himself involved. Maybe one of them was Marcia.

'All right,' he said to her—he knew she had lied to him, and she knew he knew. 'Tell me this, this way you won't betray anybody or give anything away—if Jack wanted to, would he be able to tell Porcia where the pictures are?'

'How do I know? Why shouldn't he be able to?'

'Who else is in this deal with Jack, Marcia?'

'Look, Sammy, you come here and tell me a story, how do I know it's true? How do I know you're not after the pictures yourself? You said it could be anybody putting the pressure on Jack, and *anybody* includes you.'

'If you don't believe me, get on the phone to Wallace, Jack's lawyer, in London, and ask him what I'm doing here.'

There had been no dramatic finale to their romance; they had just mutely, mutually agreed that while Jack was in trouble they ought to cool it. Big Jack had been the closest approach to a father Latch had ever known, and Latch's feeling for Marcia had always been contaminated by a sense of shame and guilt that was recharged every time the thought of Big Jack occurred to him. For this reason it had been a relief when the affair fizzled out and died; but he had never got over her or got used to being without her, and he wondered now whether it had been the same for her, and did she still want him as much as he did her.

'I'm sorry,' she said, looking down at her empty glass.

31

He took the glass from her and then she said, 'I'll get them,' and took both glasses back from him. 'You're giving me the willies creeping around the walls.' She went to the sideboard and while she was pouring the drinks, said to him over her shoulder: 'If you want to take me to South America, Sammy, I'll go. But not to get away from the Mafia.'

He went and stood close behind her, holding her arms. 'Thanks,' he said.

She turned and put her arms round him and he held her, kissing her neck and eyes and the side of her face.

'I'll go anywhere with you,' she said.

'I know,' he said. 'But we've got to find a solution to this other problem first, and South America isn't it.'

She turned from him, picked up their drinks and handed him his. 'So what do you suggest?' she asked.

He turned away. He needed time to think. There seemed to be no more point in subterfuge; but it might also be wise to keep the real reason for his presence here quiet. 'Can we meet somewhere, accidentally? Just sort of bump into each other, out in the open. I'd rather nobody knew why I'm really here, you see? Not even your very good friends down at Bandol. I just happen to be down here on holiday and we just happen to bump into each other.'

'All right,' she said. 'I'll get Freddie and Doreen and we'll go down to Cassis for dinner. The Café Malaquaise on the Vieux Port. We'll probably get there about ten.'

He looked at his watch again. He finished his drink then slowly turned to face her. 'I'll see you tonight then,' he said.

32

'Don't go, Sammy,' she said.

'It'll be daylight soon,' he said. 'I don't want anybody to know I've been here tonight.'

She looked at him, wearily, exasperated. 'The same old story,' she sighed. 'Only when we're out of the country, Marci, Jack must never know, Marci. Well, we're out of the bloody country now.'

'Now,' he said, '*nobody* must know.'

'What's wrong with me, Sammy? Am I getting old and fat?'

'If we don't work this right, sweetheart,' he said, 'you might not live to get old and fat.'

She stood still and silent, watching him.

'I'll see you tonight,' he said, and kissed her and went to the lift.

'All right,' she said.

He smiled at her trying to make it reassuring, then he pressed the down button.

7

When he got back to his hotel in Marseilles that morning, Latch booked a call for 2 p.m. to the lawyer, Wallace, in London. Then he went to bed and slept till 2 p.m. when the call came through.

Wallace said, suspiciously, 'Hello?'

'It's not on,' Latch told him. 'She won't budge and I don't blame her. Wherever she goes, Porcia's outfit can find her. There's no point in her running.'

'What do you suggest then?'

'We've got to find out who's screwing Jack. Can you get in to see him in Parkhurst?'

'Only on visiting days, once a month, through a mesh grille with a screw standing behind him.'

'You're his bloody lawyer, aren't you? Can't you see him privately?'

'Only if I can prove to a magistrate that I've got grounds to appeal against his sentence or conviction. Why? What's the problem?'

'Could his wife see him privately?' Latch pressed.

'If she had good enough reason. Like a family emergency or crisis of some kind.'

'Well, this is a family emergency. Fix it for the day after tomorrow, Wednesday. Marcia will fly to London tomorrow.'

'What's the emergency, Sammy?'

'She's emigrating to Australia. She wants to say good-bye.'

Latch hung up. He had a meal and a few drinks and in the evening drove down to Cassis. The old port was jam-packed with happy holidaymakers, mostly young and in shorts or jeans and weirdo hats, ambling around the pavé waterfront arm in arm, singing, hooting, cavorting, teeth pearly against suntans dark in the diffuse night light. They sat at sidewalk tables drinking, feet up on chairs, long legs spreading everywhere like the tendrils of monstrous succulents on the floor of an exotic swamp, or they frugged frenziedly in the roadway to snatches of beat music blazing from wide-open café juke-boxes, or they lounged on the harbour wall and watched the torpid river of humanity flowing by. A little white Fiat klaxoning shrilly, barking through its tiny exhaust pipe, tried to force a passage through the herd but was ground down to the herd's own pace. It was a warm, still night and the harbour lights and the lights of the moored boats reflected with hardly a ripple from the surface of the black water.

The Café Malaquaise, like every other bar-restaurant around the harbour, was packed with boozers, feeders, and slaves of other classic passions. The gourmets with great napkins around their necks, tucked with naked fingers into disembowelled lobsters, sucking the juices off their hands, smearing their drooling jowls, watching ravenously as it dripped from their colleagues' chins. Sweating waiters ferried in provisions and ferried out tons of used utensils, the crockery as clean as Palestine after a plague of locusts. Latch eased his way between the banks of eaters, looking for Marcia, but she was not there. He went on and up some steps at the rear into the bar section and ordered a *demi*. This section was also pretty crowded, but not so thickly as the vomitorium in front. A man in a black shirt and a straw boater was playing the piano . . . 'Every little breeze seems to whisper, Louise . . .' with a yellow cigarette on his lower lip, and a crowd of Nordic drunks at a table near him was singing, but not the number he was playing.

Latch was on his third beer when Marcia came in, followed by a woman of her own generation and a man of her father's.

She did not spot him at the bar, camouflaged as he was like a tree in a forest, among the other drinkers. She and her friends, whom he fancied he remembered from the Sundowner, were shown to a table which was already occupied by about seventeen gluttons busily stuffing themselves who did not miss a chew or a suck while they shoved around closer together to make room for the three new chairs. Latch finished his drink and had another and finished that. Then he paid his bill and headed for the exit. He was forcing through the press when she spotted him and stood and called to him.

'Marcia!' he said in astonishment.

'Sammy,' she called across the heads between them, 'Sammy Latch.'

He altered course and headed for her, pushing between the hunched backs of diners like a second-row forward with a rugby ball barging through a ruck.

'My God, Sammy, what are you doing here?' she asked, as if he was really the last person on earth she had expected to meet. She put her arms round his neck and kissed him.

'Fancy meeting you,' he said in wonder.

36

'Of all people,' she said, turning to her friends.

Lord Norwood had risen.

'Sammy, you remember Lord and Lady Norwood, don't you?' Marcia said.

'He doesn't, but no matter,' the old boy said. 'Good to see you again, Latch, anyway. I'll get you a pew.'

Doreen Norwood was smiling up at Latch from her seat. 'The one and only Black and White Sammy,' she said to him.

He smiled and nodded at her.

Norwood was a slender old man with a grog-blossom nose over silver mustachios that linked up with his fluffy silver sideburns. His wife would have been twenty-five years his junior, a good-looking woman, but with a somewhat scatty air about her. She was probably an ex-haute-couture model, and she was probably neither his lordship's first wife nor his first haute-couture model.

The old boy was bellowing at an already overburdened waiter in Hampshire County French: 'I say there, garçon, aportez une autre chaise over here, there's a good chap.'

Again the gourmandisers squeezed around without interrupting play, moving their platters along with their elbows.

Latch sat down and Marcia asked him, 'What on earth are you doing here? Are you working down here?'

'Just taking a break,' he said.

A waiter was holding a menu in front of Latch.

'Just tell him what you *don't* want,' Norwood said, 'easier that way.'

'I won't eat,' Latch said, 'thank you very much, I prefer to booze.'

37

The old boy gave a hoot of mirth.

'I'm afraid that's the old Latch style asserting itself,' Marcia said to Doreen Norwood. 'He would never pass up a pint of porter for a pound of Porterhouse.'

The other woman smiled sweetly, looking at Latch. She had dark red hair and a seemingly perpetual knowing sort of grin that unsettled Latch somewhat.

'A most fortuitous encounter,' old Norwood said. 'How long are you here for, Latch?'

'A couple of weeks.'

'Jolly good. Now old Marci will have no more excuses for playing gooseberry.'

'What does that mean?' Latch looked at Marcia.

'It means,' Doreen Norwood said, 'that she's had about one thousand offers from some of the most eligible men on the Côte d'Azur, all of which she's refused on very minor grounds.' She looked at Latch. 'Now I know why.'

'Dorrie,' Marcia said, 'if you don't shut up, you're going to get a sauce bearnaise shampoo.'

'But, darling, I too would have held myself continent for a cross between Wolfgang Amadeus and Sugar Ray Robinson who has the added advantages of being neither Kraut nor black.'

Under the table, Latch felt Lady Norwood's knee against his thigh. Above the table, Marcia leaned forward and put her hand on his forearm.

'It really is good to see you, Sam,' she said. 'Incredibly good.'

8

'Never saw you fight, Latch,' Norwood said, dabbing his moustache with his napkin. 'But I hear you were once in the ring.'

'Once,' Latch admitted. 'Or twice.'

'Why on earth do you do that?' Doreen Norwood asked. 'It looks such hard work.'

Latch smiled at her, moving his leg out of range of hers.

'I don't want to see you fight,' she said. 'I want to hear you play the piano.'

'Where are you staying?' Marcia asked him.

'In Marseilles,' he said.

'J'aime pas Marseilles,' Doreen said, lying back in her chair, 'Marseilles n'a pas l'élègance de Paris. Sammy, why don't you come down the coast and stay with us? We have our own beach, we have a swimming pool, we have hot and cold sauna-bath attendants, we have—what else do we have, Fred?'

'We have money and position, ole gel,' Norwood said gravely, 'without which you would not be allowed to behave in public the way you do.'

Doreen giggled. She was pretty drunk. Then, leaning forward with her elbows on the table, she said to Marcia, 'Look, why don't you two young things toddle off on your own if you want to, and come back to the house later for a drink and a swim?'

'Dorrie,' Marcia told Latch, 'is a congenital romantic.'

'So I gathered,' Latch said, as, once again, the red-head's leg found his.

'Well, if you're staying,' Doreen said to him, 'you're going to play the piano.'

Back in the drinking room the man in the black shirt was still toiling over the instrument.

'Do you think he'll let me?' Latch asked her.

She nodded and sat back, smiling at him. 'The philosophy, which I learned from dear old Fred here, is if you make a big enough bloody nuisance of yourself you'll get whatever you want just for shutting up.'

Would that philosophy apply, Latch wondered, if whatever you wanted was a Goya and an old master? But surely Lord Norwood was hardly the type to enter into covenants with a man like Franco Porcia. If Lord Norwood wanted a Goya or an old master, he would go to Sotheby's and bid for one or t'other, loudly and openly. And having secured it he would give it to the National Gallery and write a letter to *The Times* which he would sign 'Pro Bono Publico'. Even though he did live in the south of France.

Doreen excused herself and headed towards the rear of the establishment. Presently from the bar her pervasive contralto was heard to drill through the heavy rumble of conversation, mastication, and general flatulence.

'Mesdames et Messieurs!'

She was standing with arms upraised commanding attention. When she had enough of it, she continued:

'Ladies and gentlemen! The Café Malaquaise is

40

proud to announce that among its guests tonight is a great artist.'

Latch began to look worried.

Doreen continued: 'The Café Malaquaise is further proud to announce that the great artist has agreed to play for us. Mister Black and White Sammy Latch!'

'The silly bitch,' Latch whispered in fright. 'They've never heard of me.'

Patchy and lukewarm outbreaks of applause were occurring; they did not know whom or what they were applauding, but following an announcement like that, applause seemed called for.

'They've heard of you now, darling,' Marcia grinned at him.

'Come with me,' he said.

'You'll kill 'em,' Lord Norwood told him, encouragingly.

'If they don't kill me,' Latch said. Marcia followed him to the piano, and when the company saw that Doreen's announcement had not entirely been a put-on, the applause became more positive. Maybe one or two of them had heard of him after all. He sat down at the piano and went straight into 'Streamline Train'. Gradually the noise died out around him, they stopped talking, even the drunks at the table next door stopped singing, as the new sound got to them. Almost involuntarily they started moving with the shuffling boogie bass, while the insistently repeating, infinitesimally varying refrain picked away remorselessly from the treble.

The French like good trad and this was real old stuff out of the bowels of old Chicago. It was black men's music but Latch was good at it which is why they had called him Black and White Sammy, and the name had

41

stuck, chiefly through the ministrations of his publicity man. But he had a way with it so that it entered into you and unsettled you, disturbed the complacent, dissatisfied the placid, made you want to get up off your backside and try out a new move or two.

When it stopped there was an almost uncomfortably long silence before the clapping started and the shouting for encores, Marcia was leaning against the piano grinning at him and he went on with the 'The Fives', and then 'South End Boogie', beginning to sweat a little and to get into the mood. The place was jamming up with people attracted in from outside by the piano. Then a girl burst through the mob around Latch and stood looking down at him. She showed a great deal of burnt brown skin and a smooth fall of black hair to the small of her back and eyes like the spread wings of a raven with a flash of kingfisher blue in them. She wore tight brief shorts and a shirt not buttoned but knotted under her breasts. At first, not seeing her, Latch played on. Then her presence encroached and he looked round and up at her and abruptly stopped playing.

She was grinning at him, her lips chapped by sun and wind and salt water. 'So it *is* you,' she said. 'Hello, Uncle Sammy.'

The audience started protesting at the break in the recital, but Latch ignored it and stood up. She had grown, and not only upwards, since she was twelve years old. 'Hello, Rachel,' he said.

Her boy friend was right behind her, the tall, slab-sided young German he had seen in the early morning outside Marcia's apartment house.

'Aren't you going to kiss me?' she asked. 'You always used to.'

He put his arms round her and kissed her, but her

42

kisses had grown up too and it wasn't like he always used to. He heard the crowd complaining, demanding that he carry on playing, he saw her eyes out of focus in close-up, closed in rapture as she kissed him, and over the top of her head he saw the German standing there watching this, not too sure whether he approved or not.

Then Rachel stepped back and introduced her German. 'Klaus von Schanze, this is my dear old uncle Sammy Latch. He's not really my uncle, of course. More of a kissing cousin to my mother.' Her eyes twinkled as she spoke. 'Which I suppose makes him a second kissing cousin to me.'

Marcia was walking away.

Seeing her, Rachel said to Latch, 'I see you've found her, old Barrett of Wimpole Street.'

'Hang on, love,' Latch said to Marcia, then, to Rachel, 'What are you doing here? How did you know I was here?'

'We were on Klaus's boat, which is moored in the harbour. Somebody came running by shouting something about Black and White Sammy playing at the Café Malaquaise. I just didn't believe it. I had to come and find out.'

'Well,' Latch said, looking from the girl to the German, 'will you have a drink?'

'Why don't you come and have a drink with us on the boat?'

'Great,' Latch said, looking at Marcia who was standing solemnly on one side. 'I'd like that.'

Marcia said, 'What I'd like to do, Rachel, is tan your backside until your teeth rattle.'

'But we'd still like to come and have a drink on the boat,' Latch said affably.

43

Marcia walked away.

'Where are you tied up?' Latch asked the German.

'Along and to the left,' von Schanze indicated the direction with a wave of his hand. 'The *Walkyrie*.'

Latch grinned. 'Out of Valhalla, I presume. I'll see you there.' Then he went after Marcia.

The crowd gave him a good hand because, even though the performance had been curtailed abruptly, he appeared to be having woman trouble and so they forgave him. He caught up with Marcia down in the restaurant heading back towards the Norwoods. He stopped her and said:

'Remember why I'm here. I want to meet these people.'

Momentarily she looked undecided. 'Freddie and Doreen won't go. They hate the von Schanzes.'

'So? Doreen invited us to go off on our own if we wanted to.'

Reluctantly Marcia nodded, then went on back to the table. He returned to Rachel and Klaus von Schanze. 'We just have to excuse ourselves over there in the corner, some friends of Marcia's.'

'You mean that dear ole mother o' mine is coming too?' the girl looked more surprised than disappointed.

Latch nodded, then smiled at her. 'You two go on. I'll find the boat.'

9

It was a sixty or sixty-five-foot cruiser, not a really rich man's outfit, more of an ordinary, dirty old millionaire's job, but bigger than the boats tied up around it and so easy enough to find. Latch and Marcia climbed down from the stone dock over the stern decking and some upholstered bench seats into a well-deck. At the forward end of the well-deck, in a solid teak bulkhead under the flying bridge, a door was ajar and from beyond it a faint light glowed and a sound of music was discernible. The door opened and von Schanze beckoned them in.

They found themselves in a deeply carpeted, sparsely furnished saloon. The light was dim, as was the music, and the sense most immediately affected was that of smell; the place reeked of pot smoke. There was a group sitting on cushions on the floor to one side, at least two members of which were sucking on long, thin pipes, and looking stricken. A woman approached Latch and Marcia. She was tall and well moulded and wore a floor-length robe through which, with the light behind her, her naked body was silhouetted.

Klaus von Schanze introduced her. 'My wife, Raejean.'

'So you are little Rachel's mother,' Raejean said to

Marcia. Her voice, husky and dreamy, indicated to Latch that she was sky high on something, presumably pot. Incongruously her face was that of a high-school co-ed, freckled, plump, and innocent, surrounded by stiff, urchin-cut, blonde hair.

'Tell her what you would like to drink,' von Schanze said, then shrugged and added, 'or smoke?'

'You'll have the gendarmes in here before the night's out,' Latch told him, nodding at the blue smoke lazily curling. 'You can smell that halfway up the wharf.'

'Nothing to do with me, my friend,' the German said, indicating his wife. 'It's her boat, her friends, her pot.'

Raejean von Schanze grinned at Latch. 'If you would come in, I'd be able to shut the door and turn on the air-conditioning.' Then she turned her sunny, glazed smile back to Marcia. 'I'm sure you don't want to indulge, Rachel's mother, so I'll offer you a drink. What'll it be?'

They told her what they wanted and she floated away, naked and sinuous under her long shift, to fetch it.

Latch and Marcia stood together in a corner with their drinks, eyeing the assembly.

'Well?' Marcia asked him. 'What do you think of my daughter's friends?'

He didn't answer. But he knew that if old Jack had caught his little girl amongst this lot, he'd have taken the place apart with his teeth.

'Do you think, as her legal guardian,' Marcia pressed him, 'that I have reasonable cause to object?'

He was saved the effort of answering by Klaus von Schanze and Rachel joining them. The man was draped around the girl's shoulders, grinning vacantly.

'Hey, Sammy,' von Schanze said, 'you know back

46

there at Cassis, in the café there, when I saw you kissing my girl here I thought maybe I have to kill this bastard, maybe.'

Rachel was grinning too. Von Schanze's arm was round her neck and the hand down the front of her cupping the breast on that side. The knot in her shirt was undone and the shirt hung open and she had no bra on under it.

'She was kissing me too, remember,' Latch said.

The German laughed. Then he said, 'I know you are an old friend. Rachel has explained it to me, you are like her uncle to her. Okay, you kiss her when you meet her, you kiss her when you say goodbye.' The grin broadened. 'But you don't kiss her in between. Otherwise, I do kill you.'

This German was beginning to annoy Latch. He looked at Rachel. 'You think he could?'

'Oh Sammy, he's kidding you,' the girl said. 'Don't take everything so damn seriously, Uncle dear.'

To von Schanze Latch said, 'How does your wife feel about your girl here?'

'Raejean? I tell you, just between you and me, Sammy, you may kiss Raejean, any time you like. You may do anything you like to Raejean, and I will not object. Nor will she.'

'Do your shirt up,' Marcia said to Rachel, stiffly.

Rachel smiled at her. 'Maybe I'll do it up, maybe I won't. Maybe I'll take it off.'

The German was laughing again. 'Have another drink, Marcia,' he said.

Marcia said to Latch, 'I want to go.'

He took her arm and moved her away from von Schanze and the girl. 'You want to go and leave Rachel here?'

'What else can I do?' she asked. 'If we take her with us, she'll only be back here at the first opportunity, or somewhere else with him.'

'You thought about the law?' he asked. 'Making her a ward of court?'

'That would only alienate her completely. They'd probably run away together, abroad, and I'd never see her again.' She turned from him, with her head down. 'It's all my fault, Sammy.'

'Why is it your fault?'

'Whenever I start lecturing her about von Schanze, she throws you in my face. What right have I to lecture on this subject when I've been cheating on her father all these years with you.'

'The insolent little bitch,' Latch whispered in sudden anger. Then he said, 'You've got every right to lecture her, Marcia. It's not part of her province to question your behaviour, it's none of her bloody business; but hers is yours, legally, you're legally responsible for her.'

She smiled at him weakly. 'Don't do as I do, do as I say,' she said.

He looked away. He had to admit she had a point. He felt forked and angry. But he also felt that what he had done with Marcia might have been wrong, but not as wrong as what Marcia's daughter was doing with this German. Latch and Marcia had been over twenty-one when they'd started, and they'd started because they had loved—still, he hoped, did love—each other. He doubted that Rachel's motive was so noble, her boy friend's certainly wasn't, and the girl, he felt sure, was doing it solely out of spite. She needed a damn talking to, not from her mother, from a man, and as her father could not do it, and as Latch was so intimately involved, it looked like his job.

48

He said to Marcia, 'We're leaving, but she's coming too.'

Marcia looked at him. Rachel and von Schanze were frugging on the carpet, her shirt flying loose behind her, her breasts bare. Latch went to her and gripped her left wrist. She stopped in mid-frug and stared at him.

'We're leaving now,' he said to her.

'Well,' she said, trying to free her wrist, 'goodbye.'

'All of us are leaving,' he said, tightening his grip on her wrist.

'Oh now wait a minute, Mr Latch,' the German said, standing with his feet apart, facing Latch, and his fists down by his sides. 'Take your hands off her.'

'We're going, von Schanze,' Latch said, 'And if you interfere, I'll bust you open.'

'Oh yes?' the German grinned, intrigued, and came at Latch.

The girl shouted, 'No, Klaus, leave it . . .'

'You'll bust me open?' the German said, still grinning, still coming on, and then he took a swing at Latch.

Latch did not even shift his feet, just moved his head so that the punch missed. It left von Schanze wide open for a rip in the kidneys, but Latch resisted it. The other man looked up, momentarily puzzled as to how his fist could have failed to connect.

'I'll bust you open,' Latch assured him.

'Klaus,' the girl tried to intervene again, 'he used to be a pro.'

Von Schanze forced the grin back. 'Oh yes?' he said. Then he went on, watching Latch, 'I still want to see him bust me open. Or try. He would be the first man ever to do that.' He was moving in again for another shot.

Latch said to him, 'Listen, you stupid bastard, she's

warned you. You're not yellow if you back off. Just sensible.'

The German grinned and came suddenly, and this time Latch had to react, moving to one side to avoid the attack, and then putting his left into von Schanze's midriff. It was not a good punch, in the sense that it was far too low for the purists, but it had the desired effect in that it deprived the big German of all desire to do anything but lie down and double up and turn purple.

Rachel howled an obscenity at Latch, but Raejean von Schanze screamed: 'Now kick him! Kick him in the guts!'

Latch took hold of Rachel and dragged her out. With Marcia following, he hauled the girl along the wharf to where he had left his car.

10

Marcia drove and Latch occupied the passenger seat holding Rachel on his lap. The girl sat stiffly with her head lying back on his shoulder, her eyes closed, her face devoid of expression.

'I don't know what you hope to achieve by this,' Rachel said. 'He'll be out looking for me within half an hour.'

'He won't be out looking for anybody for a day or two,' Latch told her, knowing that, by chance rather than intent, he had really hurt Klaus.

'However long it takes him, Sammy,' the girl said, 'he'll be looking for you. And next time he'll be ready.'

Latch nodded; her words were wise. The belt in the gonads had been the least of the wounds he had inflicted on the German—the major one was to the man's pride. That one would never heal.

'Next time,' Rachel said, 'he'll kill you.'

Quite possibly, Latch thought, experiencing a sudden urge to return to Newcastle upon Tyne and resume his job at Romano's of that city.

Marcia said, 'I don't want to go back to the flat, Sammy,' even though she was driving in that direction.

'We're expected at the Norwoods', aren't we?' he said.

Rachel started laughing. 'Oh, Freddie and Doreen,' she yelled, 'oh sweet Jesus, Harry, and King George, you are priceless, Mother. Let's go to Freddie and Doreen's then, let's,' her shirt was flying open and her breasts were bare, 'and let's I walk in there with my tits all bare and say "Hallo Uncle Freddie, Hallo Aunt Dorrie, here am I with my tits all bare". Oh let's.'

'Do your blouse up!' Marcia screamed at her daughter.

In the backrush of the car's slipstream, Rachel's hair whipped across Latch's face. He moved his face out of the way of it, while trying to hold the girl's wrists and pull her shirt down to cover her chest.

Rachel said to him, 'Oh you're ever so bloody noble, aren't you, Sambo.'

'Rachel,' Marcia said, with menace, 'if you don't shut up, I will smash every tooth in your head.'

Rachel made to start again, but Latch tightened his grip on her right wrist, bending against the bone, and she jerked back with the sudden, surprising pain.

'Quiet or I'll bust it,' he said against her ear.

Marcia was in a hell of a state. They were coming down into La Ciotat and she said, 'Where, Sammy? Where shall I go? Shall we go to Freddie's, then?'

He knew she wanted to go to Freddie's and he reckoned it was because the apartment she lived in was so barren and impersonal and at the other place there was comfortable old, safe old Freddie, and the servants for protection, and Doreen, if not a friend, a contemporary, a sister under the skin, and some noise and light and motion, and people she knew, that she could talk to.

'Go to Freddie's then,' he said.

Marcia had a problem; that apartment of hers looked

hardly touched by human hand and yet once places she lived in really had looked lived in. There was nothing of her in that apartment, no indication that she had ever even dropped in there for tea let alone to live, and he'd heard Rachel say that she'd practically been living with the Norwoods. Loneliness? She had no reason to be lonely; Doreen Norwood had said she'd been getting plenty of offers.

Was Rachel the problem? Or Jack being inside? Or was it even Latch himself? He couldn't tell, he couldn't read her now, they'd been adrift too long, and she had changed. The change was subtle; but in a way, he was coming to realise, profound. He had, however, believed her when she told him she still hankered for him; so perhaps, in due course, he would find out what the trouble was; and it was this prospect alone that enabled him to resist the temptation to go back to Newcastle.

Just before Bandol she turned off the highway onto a dirt road going down towards the Med beside a high stone wall. On the other side of the road was bush, low scrub and tough eucalypti bent and aged before their time by the Mistral, with the odd mimosa tree in bloom, and from beyond the edge of the cliff ahead the sound of the sea was audible. They came to a gateway in the wall, huge wrought-iron gates wide open, and Marcia turned the Jag in there. It was a rambling white stucco villa with a colonnade of arches over slender columns covering a tiled verandah. From within the house light glowed through the leaded glass of a series of floor to ceiling windows.

They entered through one of these windows and a man appeared in an arched opening in the opposite wall, bald and dapper and wearing the livery of a butler.

He showed them into the room where Lord and Lady Norwood reposed, which was called the den, a large room with some fine pictures on the walls and a genuine Bengal tiger skin splayed out in the centre of it. 'Mrs. Carmody,' the butler announced, 'and friends.'

'I say,' Freddie rose to meet them, 'splendid!' In one hand, he clutched a brandy glass, and in the other, the bottle.

Across the patio, in through the open french window, and across the floor, wet footprints led to where Doreen was seated on a large, leather settee. Her head was wrapped in a towel, her person in a beach-robe, and her feet were bare, and still wet.

'I've just had a swim,' she smiled.

'Will you be wanting supper, milord?' the butler inquired.

'In due course, Gainsborough,' milord said, shooing the man out with irritable inclinations of his dome.

The butler retired, closing the door behind him.

Lord Norwood poured drinks for all except Rachel, who said, when offered one, 'Stuff it.'

'Dorrie,' Marcia said, 'may we stay the night?'

'Certainly you may, providing you and Mr. Latch don't mind playing bridge all night.'

'I'll have to go back to town,' Latch said.

'Why?' Lady Norwood asked him.

'I can't play bridge.'

'Damn! All right, Latch, just in honour of you, tonight we'll play poker.'

'Honestly, Dorrie,' Marcia said, 'I don't feel like playing anything tonight.'

'Oh shit!' Dorrie said. 'Honestly!' Then she looked at the girl. 'Rachel, darling, you can play poker, can't you?'

Rachel smiled sweetly and opened up her still un-buttoned shirt. 'Strip poker?'

'Well now, there's a thing,' Lord Norwood stammered, eyes bulging, 'or two.'

'Why don't you go to bed, Rachel?' Marcia asked, sounding very tired.

'You mean you trust me? How do you know I won't climb out the window and run back to Klaus? How do you go on the vision of your darling daughter up on the route nationale waving her shirt for a hitch-hike back to her demon lover in the wee small hours?'

Latch went towards Rachel. 'Time you and I had a chat,' he said to her.

'Where would you like to have it, Mr. Latch?' the girl asked him. 'In the bedroom? Down on the beach in the moonlight? You've been banging Jack Carmody's wife for ten or fifteen years, now his daughter's of age you might as well have a go at her too.'

Latch right then was in two minds whether he should slam the little bitch in the mouth; but he controlled himself, somehow, and just gripped her arm and hauled her towards the french window.

'The cave-man approach,' Doreen observed enviously.

He took Rachel out onto the terrace where the swimming pool was, and down a couple of shallow steps from the terrace onto the lawn.

There she twisted free of his grip and said to him, 'I don't need any bloody sermons from you, you bastard.'

'I'm not going to give you any,' he told her; 'but I am going to give you a clout in the mouth if you don't shut up.'

She stood staring sullenly at him, in the moonlight, on the lawn. 'Listen, Rachel,' he said, amid the buzzing

55

cicadas and the noises of all the other little denizens of the warm night, 'I'm not down here chasing Marcia. If that's what I wanted, I'd have been down here months ago, as soon as Jack was put away.'

'What are you down here for?' she asked him.

11

Maybe it wasn't wise telling her, but hers was one of the lives that had been threatened, so he reckoned she had a right to know. Also he had formed the opinion that the only way he was going to get any co-operation out of Rachel was to give her a damn good fright.

'Your father asked me to come down here,' he said. 'In fact he's paying my expenses.'

'What?'

'I kid you not, Rachel.'

'Why?'

'Somebody is going to kill you and Marcia unless Jack spills about where he hid the pictures he stole.'

She just stared at him in silence.

'He got a note out to that lawyer,' Latch went on. 'Wallace. Wallace got in touch with me. Now listen, whoever's threatening Jack, it could be anybody. Including your friend Klaus. So you've got to be sensible, you've got to co-operate. Jack has asked me to try to keep you and Marcia alive. I might have let him down in other departments, but in this one I'm going to come through for him, even if I have to pummel you into submission.'

'You're lying,' she said to him.

'You think I'm lying, ring Wallace in London and ask him.'

She looked at him, trying to gauge him, as he stood with his hands in his pockets and his eyes deeply shadowed in the moonlight. Then she turned and hurried back, up onto the terrace and into the den. Latch followed her. Marcia looked round at them, over the back of the settee as they came in from the terrace. Doreen was sitting beside her and his lordship was occupying a large leather chair on the far side of the tiger-skin.

To her mother, Rachel said, 'I want a word with you. In private, please.'

Marcia put her drink down and followed the girl out of the room.

When they had gone, Doreen said to Latch, 'What's that all about?'

He shrugged and picked up his interrupted drink. 'How did Rachel get to meet this von Schanze character, anyway?' he asked.

'At a party somewhere, I suppose. You know how these things go.'

'Do the von Schanzes live down here or are they just visiting?'

'I don't think they really live anywhere, as such,' Doreen said. 'They have a villa at Cap d'Antibes; they spend their winters in St. Moritz and their summers on the Côte d'Azur. Not short of the pence, exactly, although I understand it's all hers.'

'Raejean's?'

'Her daddy's in tobacco, back home in South Carolina, or wherever.'

'They're sick, those people,' old man Norwood said. 'Lot of 'em like that round here, you'll find. They're all so rich and beautiful and the sun is always shining on them and the photographers are always snapping them and the gossip columns are always yapping about them and the rest of humanity envies them, so they come in the end to believe that they are a race apart, a chosen clique, inhabiting their own private Mount Olympus high above the world of mortal men. They're all pretty sick, you'll find.'

'Freddie,' Doreen said, 'no more cognac, darling, please.'

'Yes, my old boot,' her husband said to her, 'perhaps it's supper time. Are you going to change?'

'Suppose I ought to,' she said. 'Come up with me, Mr. Latch, I'll show you your room.'

He looked at her.

'Well, you want to brush up before supper, don't you?' she asked.

After a moment, he shrugged and finished up his drink. He supposed he wanted to brush up, but the thought would never have occurred to him spontaneously.

12

Marcia was sharing a room with Rachel and Latch's room adjoined, but there was an interconnecting door. About an hour after the household had retired, Latch crept into the adjoining room, roused Marcia, and told her to come into his room as he wanted a word with her. Rachel was sleeping soundly.

When Marcia joined him in his room, Latch asked her: 'How is she?' meaning Rachel.

'Out for the count. I gave her a grain of phenobarb.' She sat on the edge of his bed, sort of sagging as she sat, and there were dark rings under her eyes.

'I told her about the other thing,' Latch said.

The woman nodded. 'She told me you had. Do you think it was wise?'

'It seemed the only way to get any co-operation out of her.'

'She made me promise to tell Jack about you and me,' Marcia said.

'What?'

'And I'm going to keep it, Sammy. I'm going to London tomorrow and see Jack.'

So guilt was her problem, Latch thought. The reason she couldn't live in her own apartment at La Ciotat was because she couldn't stand her own company, she soured her own taste. It had affected him too, but not as seriously as this. Her guilt, of course, was compounded by Rachel; Marcia had more than deceived Jack, she had neglected her daughter, in Latch's favour.

'Listen, Marcia,' he said. 'The reason I just woke you up and got you in here was to tell you I want you to go to London tomorrow, and to see Jack. In fact I've already fixed it with Wallace. But you're not going to tell Jack about us. You can keep your promise to Rachel if you must; but after this other business is sorted out. I'll tell you why, honey—because if you tell Jack now that you've been cheating him, and with me, those pictures he stole are suddenly going to seem a hell of a lot more important to him than any kind of human relationship. Do you understand? So until this threat is lifted, you mustn't tell Jack about us. Not unless you want to see Rachel dead.'

She thought about that for a moment. Then she said: 'What if somebody else tells him?'

'You mean like Rachel?' he said.

She nodded.

'You go to London tomorrow, and while you're away I'll explain exactly what the situation is to her.'

'This promise, Sammy, was her price for not seeing von Schanze again.'

'You'll keep it. I'll go with you and we'll tell him together, we'll spill the whole garbage truck all over him if that's what she wants. But not until the other problem is solved.'

'What do you want me to go to London for, anyway?'

'Wallace is fixing for you to see Jack privately. There'll be a screw in the room with you, but just to make sure you don't pass him a gun or anything.

61

He'll keep his distance, so if you keep your voice down he won't overhear what you say. Jack's got to break, or appear to, and spill the beans to Porcia. He's got to tell Porcia that I know where the pictures are, and that I've come down here to get you and Rachel off the hook by handing the pictures over.'

'So they'll have to contact you, whoever they are.'

'Yes,' he said. 'And that's all I need. Just to know who it is. Once I know him, and he knows I know him, that's it. He won't hit you or Rachel, because if he does, he knows I'll hit him.'

'It seems a pretty precarious balance to me.'

'It's the only way out I can think of. Can you come up with a better one?'

'You're putting yourself on the hot-spot, Sammy.'

'Not really. In a way, I'll be safer than any of you; they won't hit me if they think I can tell them where the pictures are.'

She nodded, and after a while said, 'All right,' and looked up at him. 'You're really worried about this threat, aren't you?'

'Jack is, so I reckon I ought to be, just a little. You think it's a bluff?'

'I think the chances of it being anything else are pretty slender.'

'Long shots,' he said, 'sometimes win.'

'Yes,' she said standing up, 'they do.' She looked beaten, exhausted, and deeply troubled.

He stood close to her holding her arms. 'We'll sort it out, honey. I promise.'

'Promises don't seem to mean much these days,' she said, 'do they?' She looked down and then said, 'It doesn't matter, anyway. Good night, Sammy.'

She left him and went back to her own room. As the

door closed between them he was thinking about women and wondering if he would ever fully understand how they worked and wishing he'd never touched a woman but had stuck to playing with himself like he used to do at school; it would have made life so much simpler.

13

In the morning Latch drove Marcia over to her apartment at La Ciotat to pack a bag and pick up her passport. After lunch they all went down to Nice, Latch and Rachel in the E-type following the Norwoods and Marcia in the Norwoods' chauffeur-driven white Bentley Continental, for Marcia to board a flight for London.

When Marcia's flight had gone, Doreen wanted to carry on to Monte Carlo to the casino, but Latch had to return to Marseilles for a shower and a change of clothes and Rachel, who had agreed to stay with the Norwoods during her mother's absence, did not particularly want to go anywhere. So they all headed back for the Norwoods', the Bentley this time following Latch and Rachel in the E-type.

As he drove, Rachel said to him, 'I take it Mother told you why she's gone to London.'

He glanced sideways at her, and then said, 'To tell Jack that she once had an affair with me?'

The girl said, 'Don't you feel you ought to have gone with her, Sammy?'

'When she tells him that,' Latch said, 'I'll be with her.'

'Then you'd better be on the next plane to London.'

'What good do you think it would do, Rachel, to tell

old Jack that, about Marcia and me? Do you think it would make him happy? Would it even make you happy?'

'It's a wrong you two have done him; he has a right to know about it.'

'He has a right to bash his brains out against a brick wall too, if he wants to. But maybe it's not a right he would want to exercise right now. Look, Rachel, your old man's got fifteen or twenty years in jail ahead of him; don't you think that's enough problems for one man for the time being? Do you really think he needs any more? Do you really think he needs to know that his wife and his friend have cuckolded him, so that he's not only behind bars for a hell of a long time, but he's got a pretty sick story to eat his guts out the whole time he's in there? Does he really need to know, Rachel?'

'You're scared of him, Sammy.'

'I'm scared, but not of him. I'm scared for your life, and your mother's, and right now Big Jack holds your life and Marcia's in the palm of his hand. If he found out about Marcia and me right now there's a good chance he'd say stuff the lot of you.' He had decided not to tell Rachel the whole truth—just as much of it as he wanted his unknown enemy to know. 'That's why she's not going to tell him about us at this time, Rachel,' he went on. 'Even though she promised you, I know. She'll keep that promise, and when she does I'll be with her. But not just yet awhile, because for the moment your life is at risk. She's gone to London and down to the Isle of Wight to Parkhurst jail to see Jack and beg him to hand over the pictures to whoever's threatening you. When the threat is lifted, we'll spill the beans about the other thing if you insist.'

65

'You bastard!' she said, turning in the bucket seat to face him, 'you talked her out of it.'

'Can't you see why, for God's sake? He just might not feel inclined to hand over a few million quids' worth of pictures to save a woman who's been deceiving him.'

'So you're deceiving him again,' the girl said.

'To save your life, for Christ's sake, can't you understand that?'

She sat back in the seat with a face like thunder. 'Yes,' she said slowly. 'I understand.' And for the rest of the ride back to the Norwoods', she remained silent.

He arrived at his hotel in Marseilles about 10 p.m., put the car in the basement, went up to his room and sat on the bed. He had had a long and exhausting drive and he lay back on the bed to stretch, thinking about having a shower and going out for a meal somewhere, and when he woke up it was 4 a.m. He had the shower then and went to bed and slept till nine. There was a cable for him from London:

ARRIVED OKAY LOVE MARCIA

He read it several times, over breakfast, especially the bit that said 'love, Marcia', wondering if she meant it or was just being courteous in cablese. Then when he had eaten, shaved and dressed, he headed back for the Norwoods'.

As he pulled up below the verandah, Doreen rushed out of the house and said to him: 'She's gone.'

Presumably, she meant Rachel. 'Gone where?' he asked.

'God knows. She didn't come down to breakfast, so I sent a tray up to her room and she wasn't there. Her bed hadn't even been slept in.'

66

Unlike your bed, Latch thought, looking at her, for she was wearing a quilted house-coat, no make-up, and a band around her head to control her undressed, deep auburn hair. Her bed had obviously been well slept in.

He didn't bother to get out of the car. 'Where's von Schanze's boat?'

'We don't know. Freddie's checked all the way along from Cassis, La Ciotat, Bandol. He's on his way down to Cap d'Antibes now to try the von Schanzes' villa there.'

Latch slipped the Jag into first gear. 'How long ago did he leave?'

'Not long, about twenty minutes.'

He let in the clutch and roared off down the gravel drive. He turned right, out the gate, then right again on to the highway, and put his foot down. In less than half an hour he was on the other side of Toulon, soaring through Hyeres and then the long string of camp-sites and the seaside shopping centres that service them all the way up to Frejus, where he joined the autoroute. Here he let the E-type do what it was built for which is to go like hell, and soon he sighted the big white Bentley with the top down floating along sedately in the distance ahead of him. He caught up and tucked in behind it, old Freddie sitting up there in the back seat in his peaked cap behind the chauffeur looking like the Maharajah of Rankipur, or something.

Realising that he was being followed, his lordship looked around and Latch waved to him. After some moments of scowling and peering his lordship recognised the driver of the Jaguar and nodded and waved back, and they proceeded thus in line astern down to Cannes, where they arrived at about 2 p.m. On the other side of Cannes, at Juan Les Pins, the Bentley turned off for Cap d'Antibes, and Latch followed suit.

The von Schanzes' villa was barely visible through a screen of trees below the road. Further down, below the house, the sea lapped timidly at a private beach, as if it were only there under sufferance. The Jaguar followed the Bentley through a wide gateway and along a drive that meandered through untended gardens that were almost jungle. The house had an air of decaying splendour, pillars gripped by gristly vines and walls covered in cascading creepers. The masonry was cracked and to mount the porch was to risk a broken ankle, at least, on the loose flagstones; but inside, the place was reasonably clean and quite palatial, despite a savage and sparse décor. Latch and Lord Norwood were shown into a room in which the walls, floor, and ceiling were all done in a zebra-skin motif. Everything in fact, apart from a huge, startling sunburst picture on one wall, was covered in zebra skin, which made the furniture difficult to find, if in fact there was any furniture.

Having deposited them here, the manservant left presumably to announce them, and Latch lit a cigarette.

'I've found a chair!' Lord Norwood announced, and keeping his hands on it to place it, sat down. He appeared to sit in mid-air.

'Extraordinary,' Latch said. 'Can you find an ashtray?'

The door opened and Raejean von Hanze entered. She was smiling her sunny, freckles-and-teeth smile, looking like a debauched version of Doris Day, and wearing a neck to ankle robe in violent saffron slit on one side almost to the waist to expose a sinuous flank above a naked leg.

'Well, well, well,' she beamed, 'Lord Norwood, how

nice to see you. And Mr. Latch, no less. This is nice. What can I do for you?'

'Is Rachel here?' Latch asked her.

'Rachel?' the woman looked puzzled, 'No. Should she be?'

'Is your husband here?'

'You know, I don't think he's here either. Don't tell me they're off again, those two star-crossed lovers.'

'Where is Herr von Schanze,' Lord Norwood asked her, 'do you know?'

'I haven't got the foggiest, Lord Norwood. Just hang on a second.' She went to the door and yelled out into the hall: 'Gunther! Gu-u-u-unther!' and presently the manservant reappeared.

'Gunther, do you know where Herr von Schanze is?' the woman asked him.

'No, madame. He received a telephone call late last night and went out immediately afterwards and has not returned.'

'Well, as long as you're with us, Gunther, you can fix us some drinks. What'll you have, gentlemen?'

'I'll have a beer,' Latch said.

'Oh, cognac,' Lord Norwood said. 'Please.'

'He's with Rachel, obviously,' Latch said, meaning Klaus von Schanze. 'Any idea where they might be?'

The woman shrugged. 'Probably on the boat, but that could be anywhere. Why don't you sit down, Mr. Latch?'

Gunther served the drinks and retired.

'Because I'm not sure whether there are any chairs in here or not,' Latch said.

'I only found this one by falling over it,' Lord Norwood said from his chair.

'You'll get used to it after a while,' the woman said.

'For instance, right here, believe it or not, there is a settee.' She demonstrated by sitting on it. 'Sit here,' she smiled up at Latch, patting the seat beside her.

Seating himself, he said, 'Haven't you any way of contacting the boat, like radio?'

'Sure; but that's not going to tell us where it is. It's not going to tell us anything, if Klaus doesn't want to answer.'

'Let's try it just the same,' Latch said.

She consulted the large watch on her right wrist. 'It's no good trying now, anyway. Not before 1800, that's the next time for private chats with the *Walkyrie*, between 1800 and 1815, this maritime nonsense you know? He won't even have the receiver switched on now.'

'I see,' Latch said.

'Anyway, Mr. Latch, what exactly is your interest in little Rachel?'

'Her mother's gone to London,' Latch said, 'and in her mother's absence I'm supposed to be guarding little Rachel's moral interests. Your old man, Mrs. von Schanze, is one of the things I'm supposed to be guarding them against.'

The woman laughed. 'And who guards them against you, Mr. Latch?' she asked.

'I,' Latch said, 'am Caesar's wife.'

She looked horrified. 'You mean you're queer?'

Now he laughed, and so did Norwood.

'No,' Latch said. 'Just above suspicion.'

She was smiling at him again. 'No, Mr. Latch. I don't think so.' Then she said, 'I tell you what, I don't know where they are now, but I could certainly find out for you. I'm sure Lord Norwood has other things on his agenda for tonight, so why don't you, Mr. Latch, come back here later in the evening, by which time I'll probably be able to tell you what you want to know.'

'Couldn't I just telephone you?' Latch asked.

'You know, I'm really lousy at answering telephones, Mr. Latch?' She was looking at him straight-faced, her gaze rock steady. Her legs were crossed, the naked one nearest him, and around the ankle she wore a small gold chain. 'But don't if you don't want to,' she said, shrugging.

'All right,' he said. 'About what time?'

'About dinner time.'

'About what time is that?'

'About nine o'clock.'

He nodded. She saw them out of the house, and Lord Norwood called to Latch, as they were heading towards their respective cars: 'Follow me into Cannes and we'll have a drink.'

14

They sat at a table on the sidewalk outside a bar in Cannes and Lord Norwood said to Latch: 'I'd think carefully about going back there tonight, if I were you. She's a devious bitch, that one.'

'What option do I have,' Latch asked, 'unless Rachel shows up in the meantime?'

'She could be at home now for that matter.'

'Well, I'm going to hang around here,' Latch said, 'until it's time for my appointment with Raejean, so before I go back there this evening I'll give you a ring about eight, eight-thirty, just in case Rachel has turned up.'

'Right. Do you know the number?'

'No. Do you?'

'No. Damned if I do. But it's in the book.'

Latch said, 'What exactly don't you like about Mrs. von Schanze?'

'I don't rightly know. I just don't like the looks of her, or the smell of her, or anything about her. And him likewise.'

Latch grinned. 'But you are an old-fashioned gentleman, Lord Norwood,' he said. 'You just don't like Americans and Germans, period. America is rightly our colony and Germany is our ancestral enemy. Right?'

'Perhaps. My view may be coloured by the elements

of history; but history is merely a series of repetitions, nothing really changes in history, and there is nothing new, believe me, my boy.'

'Lies, damn lies, and statistics,' Latch said.

'Just be careful tonight,' the old man said, 'And give us a ring about eight.'

After the old man had gone, Latch sat there and drank a few more beers at fifteen new francs a time, which is what beer costs in Cannes. The old boy was right, of course; the von Schanzes were a pretty bad lot; maybe not bad in themselves, but certainly bad for a kid like Rachel. She was too young and easily impressed, malleable and pliable to be exposed to a couple of old life-weary bums like Raejean and Klaus. Why wasn't she knocking around with a bunch of kids her own age, for Christ's sake? The obvious and simple answer had occurred to him once before; Klaus was Rachel's revenge on Marcia for Latch; but he didn't believe that that was entirely the answer. Rachel, he reckoned, had a crush on Klaus; she was in love with him.

What, then, was Klaus's game? Old Santa Klaus, what the hell was he up to? He sure as hell did not have a crush on Rachel and he didn't need her body, there were half a million bodies as good as Rachel's along the Riviera and Klaus was young, good-looking, and rich enough to score with practically any one of them he wanted to. So why was he chasing after her, encouraging her, leading her on? So that when the time came—the end of the month—he would know where she was? It was an interesting theory, Latch reckoned.

And why, for that matter, was he, Latch, sitting here like a fly in a bloody cobweb paying fifteen new francs for half litres of French beer preparing to mount up and

ride to rescue a spoilt, selfish, scatter-brained little dam-
sel from a fate she didn't want to be rescued from anyway? Had he gone off his marbles or something? Why
should he care—what was the point of caring about
Rachel anyway? None that he could see, there was no
good point in it at all. Except the guilt syndrome. If she
really was trying to ruin herself just because of him and
Marcia, he did feel a certain obligation to try and stop
her. He had to try to make her see the facts, that he and
Marcia were not worth ruining herself for, that he had
not transcended her in her mother's heart, that it was
time she grew up and stopped behaving like a halfwit,
like a drunk in charge of a loaded gun, which was how
she was behaving, drunk with pique and juvenile ideal-
ism and an assurance of her own righteousness and
sense of justified grievance, all the things she was using
as excuses for carrying on like a whore's cat with this
randy Hun.

He owed it to old Jack to try to pound some sense
into her. At about eight-thirty, having killed several
hours in several bars and several fifteen new franc
beers, he called the Norwoods' number. The butler
answered, then Doreen. There was no sign of Rachel,
but a telegram from Marcia had arrived; she was
coming back tomorrow morning. Latch hung up and
went back to where he had parked the car and headed
for Juan Les Pins and Cap d'Antibes.

It was another of the Mediterranean's warm, silken
nights out on the cape with no breath of air moving
the trees or the sea below that reached out to Corsica
dyed by moonlight, smooth as a sheet of tin. He turned
in at the gates of the von Schanzes' residence; lights
shone through the wild, giant flora ahead and all
around him. The broad terrace with the swimming

74

pool to the north of the house was floodlit but deserted, a large pneumatic Loch Ness monster floating on its side in the water. Where the drive widened in front of the house, however, a few cars stood. He left the E-type among them and went up the steps and across the cracked porch to the front door, which he found wide open, so he went into the foyer. Raejean von Schanze stood a few steps from the bottom of the stair, one hand on the banister, smiling at him.

'I heard your car,' she said, by way of explaining how she had anticipated his entry so precisely. Then she said, 'Come on up,' and turned and began to climb the stair.

He by-passed the zebra-striped room and mounted the stair behind her. She was wearing an ankle-length robe of very fine gold lamé that was quite transparent and no underwear at all, her favourite rigout. Through the fine-gauge gold net he watched the muscle cording and softening in her legs as she climbed ahead of him, and she wore gold slippers and the thin gold chain around her right ankle. At the top she opened a door off the hall and ushered Latch into a room with a wood-block floor, deeply cushioned couches around the walls, and heavy drapes over the windows. He went in ahead of her and turned and saw her closing the door, and locking it.

'Is that necessary?' he asked.

She looked up at him and her wide, unpainted mouth broke into that sunshine smile of hers, but there were pouches under her baby blue eyes. 'Yes, it is,' she said, 'I'm afraid.'

Then she tossed the key of the door the length of the room. He turned, following the trajectory of the key, and saw it neatly fielded by a man who had just

75

come in through a second door. He was a tall, blond, muscular young man, naked to the waist, wearing white bell-bottoms tight enough at the top to advertise his endowments in the private parts department.

Turning back to the woman, Latch said, 'I've been suckered, have I?'

She shrugged, smiling, but uncertainly. 'You wanted to know where Klaus and Rachel were.'

He looked back at the stud bull at the other end of the room. Through the arched doorway just behind the stud bull, Klaus came in, then Rachel, then two more stud bulls, just like the first, beach-boys with suntans and biceps and bunched, hard-packed guts. Latch had walked straight into it.

Klaus's face was pale, anticipating a deep satisfaction, his eyes on Latch. The muscle-men flanked him.

Rachel stood to one side. 'Hallo, Sammy,' she said, almost chirpily. 'Remember what I told you Klaus would do to you the next time you met him?'

Latch's eyes were moving desparately in search of a weapon. All he could see was a chair that would have taken two men to get off the floor. There were the windows behind the heavy drapes; the drapes were too heavy, if he charged one of them he probably wouldn't even break the window beyond let alone go through it. To get to the one unlocked door, he would have to go through von Schanze's phalanx of studs.

He started moving towards them, as they came in towards him. 'Rachel,' he said, 'your mother will be back in the morning.'

'She can get stuffed,' Rachel said, 'and probably will; but not by you.'

There was an ash-tray on a marble-topped table by the wall.

'Latch,' von Schanze said, 'you hurt me the other night, you know, with your dirty punch; but you will never hurt me again, Latch, I can assure you.'

They were coming for him. He picked up the heavy glass ash-tray and hurled it at the left flanker and followed it while the man fell, leaping him and swerving into Klaus von Schanze who came at him, driving the German down, but the other two had him now, one from each side. He swung, bringing his right elbow around in a haymaking chop and kept going, low down, barging, ramming through with his head and shoulders; then a pile-driver landed in the left side of his back, knocking him sideways so that he lost his footing. He hit the floor and the friction of the parquet as he slid burned his face. Then they were all on top of him, subduing him so that von Schanze could get things organised.

While two of the studs held Latch, von Schanze waded in. After a while Latch was bleeding from the mouth and nose and breathing noisily. He could vaguely hear them talking, a slumbrous, grunting monologue; before the real pain came, the last voice he remembered was that of a woman, the unmistakable Scarlett O'Hara accent of Raejean von Schanze; she seemed to be screaming and close to hysteria. She was saying:

'No. No! Not his hand! *Not his hand!*'

The rush of cold air over his face halfway revived him. A stream of lights was flashing past above him, endlessly whipping by like fluorescent custard-pies. There was the roar of the cold wind surging around him, and pain, chiefly in his chest and back and thighs. After a

77

time the flashing lights above did not dazzle him. He was lying in the passenger seat of the E-type, his own car. His left forearm was resting on the top edge of the door beside him, the wrist and hand hanging over the side. The wrist and hand were numb. Bare feet were operating the gas and brake pedals, long, bare legs above them. Rachel was driving. Then, as a taste and stench of blood and vomit invaded his consciousness, he abandoned it, and went back to sleep.

She stopped the E-type at the gates of the Norwoods' villa near Bandol. Another car pulled in behind it, and neither vehicle was showing lights. The car at the back was a black Porsche. Rachel got out of the Jag, went to the gate-post and rang the house-bell. Then she scurried back to the Porsche, boarded it, and the car immediately went into reverse, roaring backwards up the lane into darkness.

The Norwoods' butler came out to see who had rung the bell. He found Latch lying in the car, his breathing bubbling in his throat. Latch's left arm was still hanging across the top edge of the door and when he looked at Latch's left hand the butler, not ordinarily a blasphemous man, blasphemed.

The Norwoods' doctor's name was Whittaker, an ex-Harley Street man who had opted for premature retirement and now ran a very exclusive clinic out on Cap Sicie; his patients were generally old friends, now geriatric cases. Freddie Norwood rang him and Whittaker said he would come straight over.

Between them, the butler and the chauffeur carried Latch upstairs and put him on the bed in the guest room. Doreen Norwood sat beside the bed in her quilted silk dressing-gown staring at the mess that had been made of Latch and feeling slightly sick. Though

78

his mouth was very bad, Latch was trying to say something to her.

'Don't talk, Sammy,' she said. 'The doctor's coming.'

He managed to mouth the words: 'No—police.'

'No,' she said, 'no, of course not.'

After Whittaker had examined Latch and treated him he joined the Norwoods downstairs in the library. He looked worried and he said to Doreen:

'Are you sure you don't want me to inform the police?'

'Not yet, anyway, please, John,' the woman said. 'Wait until Marcia gets back in the morning. I suspect that her daughter is involved in this, and Mr. Latch himself said no police.'

'He was conscious?' Whittaker accepted a Scotch served by the butler.

'Just for a moment.'

'How is he, John?' Lord Norwood asked.

'Poor,' the doctor said. 'It's a criminal case without a doubt. The fellow has been brutally beaten, so brutally that I think the police would call it attempted murder. And if, as you say, he was a professional pianist, he's also been deprived of his livelihood. He has compound fractures of practically every bone in his left hand.'

'Oh my God,' Doreen whispered.

'What did they do to his hand?' Freddie asked.

'God knows, Freddie,' Whittaker said. 'It looks as if it's been put through a mangle. I can't say exactly how bad it is without X-rays, but I doubt that he'll ever play the piano again.'

'What have you done for him?' Doreen asked the doctor.

'All I can for the moment. Immobilised the limb and given him a jab.' He consulted a gold half-hunter watch. 'He won't wake before I return in the morning, and then I shall move him out to the clinic.'

'John,' Lord Norwood said, gravely. 'I want no expense spared in this man's therapy, particularly in so far as his hand is concerned. I want you to get the best man money can buy on the job. Do you understand? I want him here as soon as possible, tomorrow if you can manage it. I'll underwrite his expenses and his fee.'

Whittaker looked vaguely puzzled. 'What is this fellow to you, Freddie?' he asked.

'What is he?' old Freddie blustered. 'A damn good pianist is what he is. Or was.'

Whittaker nodded. 'Always a tragedy when something like this happens to an artist. Was he any good, really?'

'You can hear him play any time you want to,' Doreen said. 'We have some of his records, and I can assure you he was good.'

The doctor finished his drink. 'I'd like to hear them sometime, Doreen,' he said. 'But right now I'd better get weaving. I'll try to get hold of a man called Tollinger, of Zürich, who is said to have worked miracles in bone surgery; he might not be the best in the world, but he is certainly the most expensive. Anyway, I shall go back to the house and get onto it immediately. I still think you ought to reconsider your decision about the police.'

'I want to wait until Marcia gets back for that,' Doreen said.

'As you wish,' Whittaker said. 'I'll see you in the morning, early. About seven-thirty.'

15

Latch could remember Somerset, the old men and the rough cider. The men were not really old, it was the cider, the scrumpy, that aged them early. Some of them were just in their thirties and they looked sixty. Cirrhosis would kill them before they were forty, shrivelling their livers like the sun shrivels dates. The cider was their way of dealing with life, their anaesthetic against everything, against existing. It was a way to live and sometimes it occurred to Latch that it might not be a bad way to live, no concern, no problem, no bureaucrats or battling for the inside in the bloody great rodent derby. Just sitting silently and stewing. The Rockies might crumble, the planet might bounce out of orbit, but as long as the flow of scrumpy continued nothing would ever disturb these men, no catastrophe would touch them, no urge or lust or greed or envy or hunger would drive them, no necessity would chain them to the rails, and not even death would frighten them.

Black and White Sammy had carried this memory with him all his life and it had been a comfort to him. If all else collapsed, there would always be scrumpy.

His room at John Whittaker's clinic was a good one, luxurious even, with a fine french window opening onto a terrace beyond which sprinklers turned on torpid lawns, bees explored the flower beds, and butterflies hunted in the hot, gold mornings. Beyond the gardens was the Mediterranean. It was a place where film stars came to have hammer toes adjusted and carbuncles lanced on their powdered posteriors, and the ancient rich came to be put peacefully to sleep. Latch was probably the only patient in serious need of treatment that the place had ever entertained. He was attended by a posse of starched and sterilised nurses who wheeled him around silent, frigid corridors for X-rays and physiotherapy and alcohol rubs and out onto the terrace to sit in the sun and contemplate the meaning of things. He had regular injections into his damaged hand which paralysed it and killed the pain in it. Twice the hand was examined by a portly little man who spoke with a German accent; this man, Latch understood, was going to operate on the hand, though Latch was at a loss to understand what the hell good they expected this to do. His hands were insured and in its present condition his left hand was worth at least twenty-five thousand to him.

On her return from England Marcia had visited him but she had cried and blubbered so much that he had not been able to get very much sense out of her. She had been to see Big Jack in Parkhurst, though, and delivered Latch's message. Latch asked her to go into Marseilles and collect his bag and settle his account at the hotel there, which she agreed to do.

Professor Tollinger proposed to tackle Latch's hand in a two-part operation, the first on the bones of the carpus in the wrist, and the third and fourth carpals and metacarpals; the second on the thumb and its joints and bones, and the bones of the index and middle digits. The first of these complex osteotomys was performed two days after Latch was admitted to the clinic. It was a long and intricate business but did not require total anaesthesia so that the patient, though tranquillised, was conscious throughout.

The following morning the nurse came into his room and announced a visitor. 'Ma'amselle Carmody,' she said.

'Ma'amselle?' Latch's surprise showed.

'Oui, monsieur. Will you receive her?'

'Not "madame"?'

'No, monsieur. Ma'amselle, une jeune fille.'

'Show her in,' Latch said, thinking that perhaps this was it. He harboured no more fond illusions about Rachel. She was a solid oak, bronze-studded bitch, and by now the word had had time to get from Jack Carmody in Parkhurst to Porcia in London, and back to Porcia's principals, that Latch knew where the pictures were. It would not have surprised Latch to have discovered that Rachel was one of Porcia's principals.

The girl came in and stood by the bed looking down at him. She wore tight white pants with flared legs, a black cotton singlet, and sun-glasses, which she removed.

'I'm sorry about your hand,' she said stiffly. 'I thought they were just going to beat you up a bit; I didn't realise he was going to smash your hand.'

'What exactly did he do to my hand?' Latch asked her.

'He . . .' she shuddered and turned away from him. The memory was obviously not pleasant. 'He dropped the marble table-top on it a few times.'

'Why, Rachel?' he asked. 'I mean all I did to him

83

was hit him in the belly, and not very hard at that. Why did he have to do this to me?'

'I told you that, Sammy. You hurt more than his belly when you hit him. You hurt his pride.'

'That's ridiculous,' Latch said. 'Insane.' Then he remembered some words of Freddie Norwood: '. . . they come in the end to believe that they are a race apart . . . inhabiting their own private Mount Olympus high above the world of mortal men . . .'

In clobbering Klaus von Schanze, Latch had committed sacrilege.

The girl looked around the room. 'Who's paying for this? Mother?'

'My insurance, probably,' he said.

She looked directly at him and said, 'Can they—can anything be done about your hand?'

He shrugged. 'I had an operation yesterday, and I have another one to come tomorrow.'

'I mean,' she said, irritably, 'will you be able to play again?'

'I don't know,' he said. 'You know Marcia's back?'

'Is she?'

'You didn't know?'

'Don't start on that again, please.'

She watched him go through the awkward rigmarole of getting himself a cigarette and lighting it one-handed. But when he looked up and saw her watching him, she turned her back and looked out through the window across the garden. 'It's quite pleasant here, isn't it,' she observed.

'Why did you come, Rachel?' he asked.

'To see how you were.'

'Suppose I preferred charges,' he said.

She looked around at him, but said nothing.

84

'Against Klaus,' he said. 'Would you be my witness?'

'No,' she said.

'Want a drink?' he asked.

'You got what you asked for, Sammy. You wouldn't get out of our lives, you wouldn't leave us alone and go and mind your own damn business.'

'Klaus has got some kind of a grip on you, Rachel, hasn't he? Why? Why is he so interested in you?'

'Why are you?'

'I know my motives, and they're quite innocent I can assure you. I'm talking about your boy friend. I don't understand why a very rich man of—what is he? thirty, thirty-five—should be so damn keen on a middle-class adolescent. That puzzles me, Rachel.'

'Middle-class adolescent?' she said. 'Is that what I am?'

'You're seventeen and you're middle-class, so what else are you? And he must be twice your age, and he could buy and sell Marcia twenty-five times a day and not need to count the change, so what's his interest in you?'

'For a start, Klaus isn't very rich. All the money is Raejean's. His interest in me is—the same as yours in my mother. He's in love with me.'

'Klaus isn't in love with anybody but Klaus,' Latch said. 'That's why you're an adolescent.'

'You're so bloody clever, aren't you? You know all about everybody.'

'I'm no cleverer than you. Just a few years older.'

'Sammy,' she said, 'aren't you in the least concerned about what's happened to you? You might never play again, doesn't it bother you?'

It would if I thought about it, he admitted to him-

85

self. It would probably bother me to the point at which I did something silly, like went down to Cap d'Antibes tonight and killed Klaus von Schanze; and we wouldn't want that, he thought, not a murder rap in France. What I have to do, he reasoned, is wait; wait until after the shock and pain and hate are gone so I can think rationally about it; because whatever you do about it, Latch, he told himself, you need to have sufficient wits about you to enjoy it.

'Doesn't it bother you,' he said, looking up at her, 'that somebody has threatened to kill you?'

'Not really,' she said. 'Somebody might be trying to frighten Daddy; but I doubt that they would actually carry out this threat to kill me and Mother.'

'I doubt it too; but we could be wrong, Rachel.'

'I just hope Daddy isn't taking it too seriously,' she said.

'He has to take it seriously,' Latch said. 'How do you think he'd feel if he dismissed the whole thing as a bluff and then woke up one morning and found you dead?'

That one got through to her. She looked pained, and then angry. Then she said, 'However he'd feel, I don't see how it's any of your concern; and I don't see what good you can do, if they do mean to kill us you certainly aren't going to stop them, and I still believe you're only down here to tom-cat after my mother, and I just wish to God you'd go away and interfere in somebody else's life. I'm sorry I came to see you. Goodbye.'

She walked out and slammed the door behind her. The interview had not been entirely a waste of time, he reckoned. He had managed at last to penetrate the girl's armour; she was not all bad, just very young, and like the very young, very headstrong and very certain of everything. Learning that nothing is certain and that nobody is really as he pretends to be is what is called growing up, and Latch felt that that morning he had managed to shake some of Rachel's convictions.

Marcia came to see him in the evening and he told her about Rachel's visit. Marcia said:

'Was she genuine, about your hand?'

He nodded. 'Yes. I think she really feels sick about that.'

'Then what is eating her, Sammy?'

'Somebody's working on her,' he said. 'Somebody is telling her how disgusting it is that I should be having an affair with you.'

'But you're not . . .'

'But somebody keeps telling her I am, and how disgusting it is.'

'Who?' Marcia asked. 'Klaus von Schanze?'

'Your guess is as good as mine. But the real question is why. That's the one that bothers me.'

'Why does it bother you?'

'I don't really know. I just can't help feeling it's another way of getting at Jack.'

'I don't understand,' she said.

'I can't explain,' he said. 'It's just a feeling I have.'

16

The following day Professor Tollinger performed the second operation on Latch's hand, and immediately after it the hand, wrist, and forearm were encased in plaster.

The professor told Latch: 'The plaster will be taken off in three weeks' time so that the stitching and sutures can be removed from the hand; I will have to ask you to come to Zürich for that, and it will be done in my own surgery there. At that time also I will take more X-rays and be able to prognosticate more positively, but for now I can see no reason why you should not in time play the piano again as well as you ever did. The bones have been put back together as well as it is humanly possible to do so. There is of course considerable tissue damage, but nothing so serious that time and your own recuperative power, plus therapy, should not be able to correct. You will play the piano again, Mr. Latch, but it could take five, even ten years, and then only if you adhere rigidly to my directions and those of any colleagues I may refer you to.'

Somehow that speech hit Latch harder than any of the dire but nebulous prophecies of people who didn't really know, that had preceded it. You'll never play again, they had told him, the Norwoods, Marcia,

Rachel, even John Whittaker. Bullshit, he had thought, every time they said it; but now he had it from the expert, who had seen the inside of his claw and read what was written there. Ten years, it could take; five at least, and by then he'd have forgotten everything he'd ever known and be too old to start learning again. Five years was as bad as five months, five weeks, five days, without a thing you needed to go on living, knowing you could never have it again. It was a kind of castration, a kind of tearing out of the spirit leaving a hulk, a derelict shell that had once contained Sammy Latch.

He did not cry or lash out or scream or kick, but he looked pretty grim as he hobbled to the liquor cabinet in his room and took a bottle of Scotch from it. When Marcia arrived to see him, what with the after-effects of the operation and three-quarters of the bottle of Scotch in him, he was delirious. She called the nurses and the duty physician, and after they had attended to him she stayed with him, sitting in a chair beside the bed all night. In the early morning she found herself staring at his hand locked in its dead glove of plaster and she knew why he had hit the bottle last night. Tears welled in her eyes, and she took the bottle he had started and finished it for him.

In the morning, he woke before she did. He had a vicious headache, but he was surprised and puzzled to find her there, lying forward from the chair unconscious against the edge of the bed. Her head lay on her forearm on the bed, about where his knees were.

'Marcia.' He tried to say the word softly, but it emerged as a harsh croak from his larynx. Still, she did not stir. He reached across with his good hand and patted her head, stroking her hair until she moved and

89

looked up at him. Her eyes were puffed and her lips anaemic. He moved his fingers down the side of her face. She reached up and put her hand on his and they gripped.

'Come to bed,' he croaked at her.

The venetian blind was down but the sun was so bright that it glowed through, softly illuminating the room. After a moment she stood up and unzipped her dress and dropped it. She took off her bra and briefs and came to the bed and climbed in beside him. Her breasts were about his face, cool and soft, and her body was long and cool and soft against his, shivering slightly as his mouth moved on her breasts and throat; then her legs surrounded him, coolly encompassing him, and she was a compact, firm, gently resisting mass on him, holding him to point him into her, bidding him to enter her. As he moved inside her warmly, sweetly, she said:

'This time it's forever, Sammy, isn't it?'

'Yes,' he said. 'Just you and me.'

And now the piano and the hand and the great ache receded and he was comforted by knowing that when they returned, he had a remedy. Marcia.

She was lying on her side against him, propped up on one arm, feeding him with a cigarette with her free hand because his sole usable limb was around her, and she was looking at him as if she had never seen him before, as if she had always known him as someone else and had only just discovered his true identity.

Then the door opened and one of the nurses stood there for a second in which she appraised herself of the situation before discreetly withdrawing. Marcia laughed.

'That's supposed to be a disaster,' Latch said.

Marcia said, 'I don't care about disasters any more. And I don't care who knows about us, Sammy. I wish you'd let me tell that Irish bastard in Parkhurst about us; I want him to know, and everybody else who reckons to own stock in either of us; they might not think it's right, but I know it is.' She became serious, her eyes searching his. 'It is right, isn't it?'

'Yes,' he said.

Her face came down, her mouth against his while she held his cigarette up out of the way. Then she tossed the sheet aside and got out of bed and handed him back his cigarette. 'I'm going to use your bathroom,' she said.

He watched her cross the floor and hoist the venetian blind and stand there letting the sun flood over her naked body. She might not have been as young as she was the first time he saw her like that, but she was still as beautiful, possibly even more so. Then she went into the bathroom and he heard her turn the shower on.

'Bring me a glass of water,' he called to her.

He ordered breakfast for two. After a while Marcia emerged from the bathroom dripping wet and opened the french window and stood there towelling herself in the sun.

'The gardener will be along directly,' Latch said. 'You'll make his day.'

'Promise me something, Sammy,' she said.

'What?'

'This time we mean it. No more noble speeches about Jack, and I will do no more soul-searching about Rachel. From now on there is just you and me.'

He nodded. Then he said, 'With one reservation.'

'What?'

'About Jack. I'm going to do what he asked me to come down here for.'

'Oh, for God's sake why?' she sounded annoyed. 'Now I want to do what you wanted to do originally. I want to go to South America.'

'Even if that was the best way,' he said, 'which it isn't, it's too late now.'

'But look at what's happened to you already.' She had her underwear on and was getting into her dress. 'Sammy, you're no good to me dead.'

'The feeling is mutual,' he said as she stood with her back to him to be zipped up. 'That's why I've got to do it. You see?'

The door opened and the breakfast came in on a trolley powered by the nurse. Also on the trolley was a letter for Latch. It was a large white envelope addressed in copper-plate handwriting:

M. Sammy Latch,
Clinique Sicie,
Bouche du Rhône

Marcia opened it and found it to contain an invitation card, printed in embossed purple, which she read out to him:

'The presence of Black and White Sammy Latch is requested at a night of games, Saturday, September 2, at l'Hirondelle, Cap Benat, commencing at midnight. Formal, black mask.'

She looked up at him, frowning.

'September 2,' he said, 'is two days after the deadline for Jack to reveal the whereabouts of the pictures. So it looks like we've bought you an extension.'

'What does it mean,' she asked, 'black mask?'

He shrugged. 'You sit about playing backgammon or something in deejays and black masks so that nobody knows who's there. The trouble is, with this thing,' he held up his left hand in its plaster cast, 'I'm going to stick out like a sore thumb. I won't know anybody else, but everybody else will know me. What is this l'Hirondelle place?'

'You're not going, Sammy,' she said.

'I've got to. This is it, the contact, it might be my only chance to find out who is pressuring Jack.'

'I'm coming with you, then.'

'The invitation says me. Stag.'

'Oh Christ!' She stood up and went to the window and stood there with her back to him, looking out.

'What is this l'Hirondelle place, Marcia?'

'It's a kind of floating pleasure dome, they have a restaurant, night-club, casino, and a big aquarium, lots of fish, in fact that whole damn place stinks of fish. You're walking into another bloody trap, Sammy, just as you did at von Schanze's.'

'They rent it out for private functions, I take it?'

'Presumably.'

'See if you can find out who's rented it for Saturday night, will you?'

She turned back to him, looking unhappy and worried, but knowing she could not talk him out of going. 'Do you really feel up to it?' she asked. 'You've been a week in bed now.'

'By Saturday night,' he said, 'I'll feel up to it.'

17

The clinic's resident cosmeticians worked for three hours on Latch's face on the Saturday afternoon and when they had finished he looked suntanned, fit, and reasonably well groomed; but he did not feel any of those things. During the roughhouse at von Schanze's villa he had stopped a kick high on the right thigh that was still hurting grievously and causing him to limp, and there was extensive bruising on his back and arms, not to mention that which the cosmeticians had sought to camouflage on his face. The swelling on his face had subsided, however, which made things a little easier.

Marcia unpicked the stitching in the left sleeve of his jacket, so that he could get the plaster cast into the sleeve, and once he had the jacket on she sewed it up again. Thus, if he carried his left hand in his jacket pocket, and wore the black velvet mask she had acquired for him in Toulon, there was nothing to give his identity away in a room full of men similarly dressed.

When she had finished stitching the sleeve, she took up her handbag and opened it. From it she removed her little chromed Beretta. 'Take this with you,' she said.

He smiled and took the gun and dropped it into his right-hand jacket pocket. He wished he'd had it the other night at von Schanze's; it could have levelled out the odds somewhat, and it was a comfort to him now, feeling the weight of the gun in his jacket pocket.

'You know, I've been thinking,' Marcia said. 'Do you think Rachel might have come to see you the other day to find out whether you were fit enough to attend this function tonight?'

'It's possible,' he said. The possibility had even occurred to him.

'Do you think Klaus von Schanze is behind this threat to Jack?'

'That's possible too. Now stop worrying, Marcia, will you?'

'I can't,' she said.

L'Hirondelle had been booked for the night through an agency in Paris, but Marcia had been unable to discover whom the agency represented, or anything else about the 'night of games'.

'Your mask,' she told him, handing it over.

He slipped it over his head and leered at her through it. Then he hollered:

'Hiyo, Silver, c'mawn, Tonto, we'll head 'em off at the pass.'

She followed him as he went into a ridiculous, hobbling gallop from the room and along the hallway. A nurse walking towards him stopped and gaped in horror as he went by, and Marcia said to her in passing: 'He's drunk again.'

He had a taxi waiting for him. 'I'll be in touch,' he told Marcia, and kissed her and climbed into the back seat, indicating the driver to proceed. She stood on the front steps of the clinic and watched him go.

L'Hirondelle was constructed of six or eight old canal barges locked together and tarted up at great expense

95

and in execrable taste to resemble something halfway between a Mississippi paddle boat and a Paris bordello of the *belle epoque*. The complex, a jumble of gaudy lights in the darkness, was moored at a jetty sticking out from the beach on a lonely strip of coast served by an unpaved road. As his taxi came down through the scrub and sand-dunes towards the jetty, Latch could hear the music floating up and saw an orchestra blazing away in the open air at one end of the complex where people were dancing on a floor of glass illuminated from beneath. There were cars parked along the jetty, mostly big, expensive jobs with chauffeurs lounging inside them, and many boats moored on the water below. The taxi dropped him at the end of the jetty from where a gangplank lay across to l'Hirondelle. The gangplank was guarded by two men, both in evening dress and black masks, and to one of them he showed his invitation.

The man examined the card, then gave it back. 'Go aboard, Monsieur Latch,' he said.

On the deck he was greeted by another man who indicated a doorway to him and said, 'Through there and downstairs for the bar, monsieur.'

The bar was deeply padded and carpeted, silent and gloomy. It contained several drinkers, the men all in the uniform of the evening, and the women blazes of colour among them, like birds of paradise signalling for mates, showing their breasts, showing practically everything except their faces, which were masked. Nobody seemed to be talking, and the sound of the orchestra up on the deck did not penetrate down here; the only noises came from the adjoining salon in which, through an arched opening in the end wall of the barroom, Latch could see people gambling, standing around roulette wheels or sitting at kidney-shaped tables.

Everybody, including the gamblers in the salon next door, was totally anonymous except the women, and then you would have had to have known one of them rather intimately to have recognised her.

He crossed the floor to the bar, the deep-piled carpet imparting a sensation of floating a couple of inches above the floor as he walked, and said to the bartender, 'Scotch, please.'

'Oui, monsieur.'

From this position he could see through the gambling salon to the far wall, which was covered by heavy drapes except for a section in the middle which was occupied by a huge fish-tank, brilliantly lighted from within. Exotic fish and marine flora moved languidly in the clear water on the other side of a sheet of plate glass about ten feet high by as many in length, and Latch recalled Marcia having mentioned something about the place having an aquarium in it somewhere.

'Noisy bunch,' Latch said, and smiled at the barman, who provided a comforting touch of normality in that he was not masked.

The man shrugged. 'Nobody is sure who he is talking to, so nobody talks.'

Another man walked over to the bar and stood a little way along from Latch. He was short and dapper, but that was all Latch could tell about him apart from the fact that was obvious when the fellow ordered a drink, that he was French. When he had his drink he turned to Latch and said:

'Pardon, monsieur, but is there any particular reason why you carry your left hand in your jacket pocket?'

18

'My name is Latch, if that's what you want to know.'

Under the black hood and mask he wore, all that was visible of the short, dapper man's face was his mouth and his jaw. There was a smile on his mouth.

He said, 'Ah! Excellent.'

At that moment the low murmur of talk and miscellaneous noise from the salon died out and a sudden hush blanketed both the salon and the bar-room adjoining. All attention was focussed on the big fish-tank in the middle of the far end wall. Turning to watch, Latch saw two transparent plastic hoses being lowered into the tank, one at each side; they had aqua-lung mouthpieces fitted to their ends and they were obviously attached to a compressor above the tank as streams of bubbles were pouring out of them.

Then there was a great burst of bubbles at the top of the tank and out of the explosion of disturbed water, a naked girl sank into view behind the plate-glass wall. She moved languidly down through the water, her body like alabaster against the total darkness at the back of the tank, her hair drawn tightly back around her scalp, held by a jewelled clip at the back from which it floated out in a long, snake-life, black chignon. Weird, long-echoing music was being played as the girl moved among the fish above the floor of the tank, which was of white sand from which the undulating fingers of reeds seemed to reach up trying to stroke her. For some moments Latch stood like practically everybody else in the room, breathless, watching her moving, deftly breathing from time to time from one or other of the bubbling air hoses. It was some time before he realised who she was. When it came to him, he gasped: 'Rachel!'

'Oui, monsieur,' the dapper little man said. 'I believe that is her name.'

'Why,' Latch asked, troubled, 'has she got to do that?'

The little man shrugged. 'Per'aps she enjoys it, monsieur. Some people do. It is a harmless sexual deviation known as exhibitionism.'

Christ, Latch thought, watching little Rachel, remembering her when she used to go to the convent school, in her round straw hat held on by elastic round her chin, and her smart shirt and tie and long socks—what would old Jack have said if he could have seen his little convent girl now? What would he have done? He'd have had a heart attack, for Christ's sake, he'd have vomited; he'd have murdered somebody.

To the little man at the bar, Latch said, 'So this is your night of games.'

'Part of it,' the man said. 'But the game you were invited here to play, monsieur, will be in private.'

'I thought so,' Latch nodded.

'I can assure you, Monsieur Latch, if you are sensible, no harm will befall either you or the young lady.'

A little way along the bar from them a woman was talking rather loudly, and Latch could not help but recognise her voice—Raejean von Schanze. She was

99

with a group of men, and the dress she was wearing made it obvious what the men saw in her, apart from her wit that is. She glanced back and caught his eyes and then left her friends and came towards him, walking sloppily because she was three-parts drunk, her big, half bare blebs wallowing in front of her like stranded whales in a slow surf.

'You remember me from somewhere, mister?' she asked.

'Only vaguely,' Latch said.

She grinned and snapped her fingers. 'Sammy Latch!' she said. 'The last time I saw you, you were looking pretty bilious, to say the least.'

'Is your husband with you?' he asked her.

'I'm not sure. They all look the same to me tonight.'

'Just tonight?' Latch said, and saw her eyes harden in the holes of her diamanté-studded mask.

Then she smiled again. 'I guess you owed me that one,' she said. 'Seen your little pal in there, the mermaid?'

'Yes.' He looked at the dapper little man. 'I'd introduce you, except that I don't know who the hell you are.'

'Don't bother,' the little man said, and put down his glass. 'I think it's time we went, Mr. Latch.'

Looking at the little man, Raejean said, 'You're a real charmer, aren't you.'

'See you,' Latch said to her, and she just shrugged as he followed the little charmer back through the archway into the salon.

19

In the fish-tank Rachel was still performing, and as
Latch entered the salon she executed a couple of
manœuvres which, he imagined, must have been quite
a lift for the voyeurs in the assembly. Now, however,
something else was troubling him; the pain-killer was
wearing off and an uncomfortable throbbing had set
in in his left hand. He and the other man crossed to
the far corner where the dark drapes covered the wall
in which the fish-tank was set. They slipped behind
the drapes.

The little man unlocked a door and opened it to
reveal a flight of steps leading down into darkness, like
the entrance to a blacked-out basement cinema. At the
top of the steps, the man flicked a switch to turn on
a dull blue light at the bottom, where they encountered
a row of doors with push-bar locks; on the middle pair
of doors a sign was hung, just legible in the blue glow:

AQUARIUM FERMÉ

The dapper little man pushed the bar on one of the
doors, and opened it, and beyond they entered a con-
crete-floored corridor, strangely lighted by dimly glow-
ing water; fish-tanks lined both walls and from them

101

a weird twilight, like fluorescence in the sea, mottled the surfaces of the place with pale webs of undulating light. The fish from their tanks watched the two masked men proceed along the corridor.

The corridor opened into a large chamber, where the glass prisons of the aquarium's tenants were dominated by one very big tank—from the salon now, they were on the far side of the tank in which Rachel was performing.

Brilliant light from the big tank spilled back into the chamber, and Latch found that, besides himself and the little man who had brought him here, there were three others present. One sat on top of the tank that contained Rachel, from where a faint, dull rumble was audible—the engine driving the compressor up there. The other two, both men, masked and wearing the uniform formal dress of the evening, stood on the floor in the centre of the chamber, and one of them was smoking a large cigar.

Latch cursed to himself and at himself, wondering how in his maddest frenzy he could ever have imagined that these men would have agreed to meet him in the open. Here he was alone with three of them—four counting the one on top of the tank—in a place which, surrounded by water, was as effectively sound-proofed as if it had been a mile underground. And he was no closer to knowing his adversary than he had been before he left the clinic.

The men were standing there, a tall one and a short, stout one who was the one with the cigar, watching the girl gyrate in the tank above them. Once she turned and faced them, but they did not move, knowing that even though she appeared to look straight through the glass at them, she could not see them. From the water that glass wall was as opaque as stone. From here, however, Latch could see that Rachel was presenting her show from one half of the tank only; the other half was blacked out and would have been covered on the salon side by the drapes that hung over the rest of that wall. A metal grille of some description seemed to divide the lighted section from the dark, and for a second Latch was puzzled by the arrangement.

But then the dapper little man called the meeting to order. 'Mr. Latch,' he said, 'you have some information to impart.'

'You want to know where some pictures are,' Latch said.

'That's correct.'

In the high, dim vault their voices rang while, over the floor and the figures of the men, delicate nets of light moved, bent and split by the slight motion of the water in the tanks that surrounded them.

'And if I tell you?' Latch said.

'Then you and the Carmody women are off the hook. You can all live happily ever after.'

'I need more than that,' Latch said, gritting his teeth with the pain now burning in his left hand, 'before I talk.'

'What more do you need?' the dapper little man asked.

'I need to know your names and see your faces,' Latch said.

The little man looked at his two companions. The fat man gazed back at him implacably through the eye-holes of his mask. The tall one put his hands in his pockets and hunched his shoulders for a moment before arching his back, as if trying to iron out a kink in his spine, and suddenly Latch realised that

103

perhaps he knew that man; the hunching of the shoulders and the arching of the back was a mannerism he had seen Klaus von Schanze indulging, and the man was of the right height and build for von Schanze. If the tall one was Klaus, who were the other two? The fat man with his lips pursed around the soggy end of his cigar, and the short, smart, neat little man whose manners were perfect and whose manner was as hard and sharp as a carpet tack.

In the dim light, Latch saw the little man's mouth below his mask widen in a smile. 'I'm afraid that's definitely not on,' he said.

'Then go to hell,' Latch said softly.

'Come over here, Mr. Latch,' the little man said. 'There's something I want you to see.'

They went to the wall below the big tank, at about the middle where the division occurred between the illuminated section in which the girl was, and the blacked-out half. Here a steel ladder, set in the concrete floor, gave access to the top of the tank, and in the wall below the glass were several banks of electric switches.

'These switches,' the little man explained, 'govern the lights in the tanks in here. The switches in this top row govern the lights in the big tank above us here, in which the girl is performing for us. By throwing all these switches, I can plunge her into total darkness in there.'

Latch just watched him, wondering what was coming.

'Now look here.' The little man moved along to the blacked-out section of the tank.

Close up to the glass now, Latch could just see through into the dark water palely lit by the glow from the adjoining part of the tank. On the sandy floor there,

104

in the gloom, rested a monstrous head. Apart from tiny, porcine eyes, the head was almost entirely mouth, and from the head the body of the thing, thick as a man's thigh, disappeared back into the darkness at the other end of the tank.

'A conger eel,' the little man said. 'A favourite with patrons of the aquarium. His name is Victor Hugo, or maybe it is Jules Verne, I forget. He is of course one of the most voracious beasts alive, and he has not, I am told, been fed for about three days. This one is almost four metres long, a giant of his species. Now, Mr. Latch, observe the partition between his domain and the girl's half of the tank.'

Latch looked at the heavy-gauge metal grille that divided the tank.

'The grille can be raised electronically,' the little man continued, placing his hand on a short lever in the upper row of light switches, 'simply by depressing this lever. Now, Mr. Latch, think. The conger is a creature of darkness, he can see in the dark. Rachel Carmody cannot. The eel is in his element: darkness, deep water. I black out Rachel's section of the tank, and I raise the grille. The girl will be dead within one, at the most two minutes; either mauled to death by the conger, drowned, or simply as a result of cardiac arrest induced by terror—she will have died of fright. None of them, I think you will agree, a particularly pleasant way to die.'

'Who talked her into this—performance, anyway?' Latch asked, hoarse with anger.

'You asked a similar question out in the bar,' the little man said. 'It was then and still is purely academic. Now, are you going to talk?' His hand was on the lever that raised the grille partition in the tank, and, watching Latch, he covered the row of eight switches with his forearm, ready to plunge Rachel into darkness.

'All right,' Latch said, 'hold it.'

'Talk, Mr. Latch.'

'The pictures are in a strong-box in a bank vault in Zürich,' Latch extemporised.

The little man nodded, his lips drawn back from his teeth in a smile of profound dissatisfaction. 'I thought so,' he said. 'A con-trick, and a crude one, Mr. Latch. You have no more idea of where those pictures are than I do—in fact I have more. It's Sergeant Schuler's grave I want to know about, monsieur, and if you can't tell me about it, Rachel Carmody is going to die now; and if Jack Carmody still persists in playing silly games, his wife is going to die also, in the very near future. Sergeant Schuler's grave, monsieur! How do I locate it?'

The question of course completely bamboozled Latch. He glanced briefly at the other two men, the tall one doing his hunching and arching of the back thing again and the fat one with his cigar standing as dispassionately as a cow chewing her cud. Slowly the little man was depressing the lever. The bottom crossbar of the metal grille in the tank disturbed a little cloud of sand as it lifted clear of the floor and began to rise.

'Don't think this girl isn't expendable to me, Latch,' the little man said. 'Don't make the mistake of thinking that.'

The primeval head of the conger was wavering very slowly through an arc of some ten degrees, just above the bed of the tank.

Latch reached into his jacket pocket and took out the Beretta and aimed it at the little man.

'Stop it,' he said, breathlessly, 'or I'll kill you.'

106

Immediately the little man brought his forearm down across the light switches and the lights in the big tank went out; instantly and until their eyesight readjusted, everybody in the chamber was blind. Knowing they would try to rush him, Latch dodged sideways and fired into the darkness, three times; then he waited, breathing rapidly, while his vision returned in the ghostly blue light from the rest of the fish-tanks around the walls.

One of his slugs had starred the heavy glass and ricocheted, but the other two had punctured the wall of the tank in the section containing the big eel and water was jetting in two fine downward parabolas from the neat holes while cracks leapt fitfully outwards from the holes across the glass like lightning frozen against a murky sky. The little man was crouched against the wall below the tank, down on one knee. Above and behind him, a pale wash in the blackness, was the girl, suspended in the water, evidently startled into immobility by the failure of the light in her section of the tank.

There was an ominous creak as the fractured glass began to buckle under the weight of the water behind it and the short, fat man snapped: 'I'm getting out of here.' Discarding his cigar, he turned and ran, followed by the tall one, from the chamber. Then, with a loud crack, a large, jagged plate exploded out of the wall of the tank and a great cascade of water burst into the chamber. The sheet of glass came at Latch like an abandoned surfboard on the chest of a coamer, and he had to leap sideways to avoid it. The glass shattered on the concrete floor just as the cascade broke, drenching Latch and the little man who was still crouched against the wall.

In a second, Latch was up to his knees in water and now he watched as a great gleaming black coil bulged through the ruptured wall of the tank, as the sudden outrush of water endeavoured to bring the conger along with it. In the other section of the tank, Latch saw too that the drag had pulled Rachel down and slammed her against the metal grille which was all that saved her from being drawn, along with the eel, through the hole in the wall of the tank. Even so, if through panic or circumstance she was unable to get hold of one of the air-lines in there, she might still die of drowning, for despite that the tank was emptying very rapidly now, there was an awful lot of water in it to be emptied.

The water gushed from the tank in a roaring, frothing torrent, and then the conger came out; its length uncoiling it seemed to leap into the chamber impelled by the surging water. It crashed down and disappeared below the surface which was still at about knee-depth —the water must have been draining away, either into the bilges of the hybrid craft, or directly into the Mediterranean. And at the same moment as the eel landed, the little man came out of his crouch and started wading out, as fast as he could manage, after his colleagues who had fled earlier. In the tank, the girl was still pressed against the metal grille, but Latch saw that her head was above the surface now and she was endeavouring to move herself off from the grille; and somewhere, just above the floor in the dark water in which Latch stood, the conger was moving.

He was soaking wet and he could feel the plaster on his left hand drooping like a loose sock in his jacket pocket. He took a step forward, expecting the beartrap jaws of the eel to clamp round his ankle as he did so; then he took another step, heading for the steel ladder that went up the side of the tank to the platform on top. Once a thick, black loop broke the surface near him, but he made it to the ladder. Water surged and slopped around the chamber and washed away down the corridor in a series of minor bores. He dropped the Beretta into his jacket pocket and began climbing the ladder one-handed.

At the top of the tank was a platform of steel grillework about three feet below the ceiling. On the platform were the compressor and the small donkey engine that powered it, which was still putt-putting away, but the man Latch had seen up here as he entered the chamber below, had gone. He had obviously taken off at the outbreak of hostilities downstairs, and he had gone via a hatchway which was still open to the starry sky in the deckhead above.

Latch crawled over the top of the ladder and for some moments lay on the steel platform on his right side, gasping, dripping wet, and in intense pain with his left hand.

As most of the water had now drained from the tank, Rachel, who was badly shaken but otherwise unhurt, was able to climb out, up the partition. On the platform at the top she grabbed her beach-robe, then crouched beside Latch and pulled the mask off his head.

She was surprised to see who it was, apparently having expected someone else. She went to the edge of the platform and looked down into the chamber, shrugging into the robe as she did so. Then she returned to Latch and crouched beside him again.

'Sammy, what in hell happened down there?' she asked him.

'We've got to get out of here,' Latch whispered, his voice hoarse.

As if to answer his plea, a voice came to them from the open hatchway above: 'Come on outa there, you damn fools, quickly! This way!'

It was a woman's voice, and Latch knew it—Raejean von Schanze's voice. Rachel helped Latch up into a crouch below the deckhead, and with assistance from both women he managed to climb through the hatch onto the open deck above. They emerged in shadow, behind the orchestra that was performing in the open air there. The music hid the noises Latch made in coming up which were mainly gasps forced from him by the pain in his hand. From the hatch, they crossed to the side of the deck from where a set of steps led down to a big float to which many dinghies and small power boats were moored. As they stepped onto it the float dipped and rocked and bumped the hull of l'Hirondelle, and the craft tied up to it swung round on their lines, grinding their gunnels. The motion almost upended Latch, who had to stand still for some moments while waves of pain coursed through him, Rachel gripping his right arm. With difficulty he climbed down into the fibreglass tender to the *Walkyrie*. The women came aboard and an attendant came across the float from l'Hirondelle and cast off for them. Rachel sat behind the wheel with Latch beside her, half-lying, half-sitting in the passenger seat, and Raejean von Schanze in the seat behind her. The girl pressed the starter and the outboard on the transom coughed and came alive.

'Take me into the beach,' Latch said, 'and for Christ's sake someone give me a cigarette.'

Raejean lit him one and, passing it across to him, said,

110

'Mister, you look in pretty poor shape to me. Why don't we go back to the boat and you can lie down for a while?'

'You go to hell,' Latch said. 'Take me to the beach.'

'There's nobody there,' she assured him. 'Klaus isn't there, just the crew boys.'

'I think we'd better go to the boat,' Rachel said, as the tender started moving, and she turned the wheel to bring it away from the float. The *Walkyrie* was anchored a couple of hundred yards out where several other vessels of her dimensions also lay.

Latch looked at Rachel and said, 'What in hell ever possessed you to get involved in that stunt in the fish-tank?'

'I was paid five thousand francs,' she said, simply, as the breeze of their slipstream began to flick at wet strands of her long black hair. 'And I need the money for a little project I have in hand.'

20

Raejean made the tender fast to the stern of the big power boat and they went on board and into the saloon. Latch sat down on a divan against the bulkhead and started shivering.

'Is there any reason why you can't up anchor and push off from here?' he asked Raejean.

'No. Why?'

'Can you run me down to Cap Sicie, to the clinic?'

'Sure, why not? I'll get them moving.' She went to a doorway in the forward bulkhead, turning to say to Rachel, 'Help yourself to the booze.'

'I'd better get him a blanket,' the girl said, 'before he dies of pneumonia.' She went into a cabin and brought out a blanket and wrapped it round Latch.

'Now I want about four fingers of brandy,' he told her.

'I don't think you should,' she said. 'You're in shock.'

'To hell with that, I want a brandy,' he said.

She shrugged and got him a brandy. Handing it to him, she said, 'There you are, but remember . . .'

'You warned me, I'll remember. You're in the clear.'

She frowned at him, uncertain of his mood.

Raejean rejoined them. 'Next stop Cap Sicie,' she

said. 'Now, Mr. Latch, perhaps you'll tell me what the hell you were doing in the aquarium.'

'You know damn well what I was doing in the aquarium,' he looked up at her, angrily. 'If you don't, ask your husband, because he was in there with me.'

She was mixing herself a martini and she looked round at him, puzzled. 'Klaus?' she asked.

From astern came a roar as the boat's engines were fired.

'Just tell him I know he was one of them, will you?' Latch said. 'I think he ought to know, because as soon as I get back to the clinic I'm going to send a cable to London, which will mean that if Rachel or Marcia or me gets hit, so will Klaus, so I think he ought to know.'

Raejean put the cocktail shaker down and crossed the room to the door they had come in by; she closed the door, thus damping down the worst of the exhaust noise from outside. 'Mr. Latch,' she said. 'Just how much have you had to drink tonight?'

'Not half enough, honey. Not nearly half enough.'

Raejean tried abruptly changing the subject, in the hope that if she ignored him, Latch would go away. 'We'll be moving in a moment,' she said, turning to the hi-fi console. 'Would you like to hear some music?'

'How come you just happened to be waiting up top by the hatch above the tank?' Latch pressed on. 'Because Klaus told you to get around there and get me out fast before the police arrived. Right?'

'The guy who was operating the air-compressor came into the bar and told me Rachel was in trouble in the tank and maybe I ought to get back there. Okay?'

'Why you?' Latch asked. 'Why should he tell you?'

'Because I hired that barge for the night. It was my party.'

113

'So you would have known everybody there?' Latch said.

'Not everybody, I'm afraid. I just did the hiring, not the inviting. I sign the cheques, honey. That's all I'm here for.'

Latch looked at Rachel. 'And who signed your cheque for the mermaid act?'

She nodded towards the other woman. 'Who else?'

'Well, now that you mention it,' Raejean said, 'that was Klaus's idea.'

'It was my idea,' Rachel said. 'I just asked him to get the job for me because I need the money.'

They heard the sea slopping along the boat's under-parts as the *Walkyrie* gathered way. Latch had finished his drink and Raejean asked him, 'Again?' but did not wait for him to nod, just passed the bottle to Rachel so that she could pour it for him.

As she was doing this, Rachel asked him, 'What exactly happened back there? Why did the lights go out in the tank, and what made the tank collapse?'

Latch explained what had happened, and for some time after he had finished the woman and the girl stared at him in silence. Then Raejean said, 'Jesus Christ Esquire,' and looked at Rachel, then back at Latch. 'Sammy old pal, are you saying there was a conger eel in the same tank Rachel was in . . . ?'

He nodded, then took a long drink. The drink was not dulling the pain, but it was helping him bear it.

'Why should they ask you where the pictures are?' Rachel said to him. 'Do you know where they are?'

'I haven't got a clue. Have you?' As he said that, it occurred to Latch that it was a lie—he did have a clue; something the little man had referred to in the aquarium as Sergeant Schuler's grave.

114

'If you think Klaus is behind this threat to me and Mother,' Rachel said, looking at him with spite, 'I can assure you you're wrong.'

'How can you be so sure?' Despite the pain now, the brandy was clearing his head, relaxing and warming him.

'Because it was Klaus that Daddy stole the pictures from,' the girl said, 'or Klaus's family, at least, and with Klaus's connivance. How do you think Daddy knew the pictures were arriving at Stansted airport at that time on that day? Klaus organised the shipment and gave Daddy the tip-off, and then picked up nearly two million dollars in insurance out of it. It was Klaus who rented the apartment for Mother and me at La Ciotat so we could get out of England while the trial and all the publicity were going on.'

'What?' Latch blinked at her.

Then Raejean laughed, her deep, lazy laugh. 'Is that what he told you, honey?'

The girl looked round at her. 'Yes. Why?'

'Because it's not strictly true.'

'What the hell are you talking about?' Latch asked. 'In the papers it said the pictures were owned by some baroness somebody...'

'That's correct,' Raejean said. 'Elena, the Baroness von Shauern-Oberhulz, who is Klaus's great aunt and only living blood relative. You might think that makes him her heir, but unfortunately for him it doesn't. She hates his Prussian guts. And it was the baroness who picked up the insurance money, not Klaus, who is, fiscally speaking, on the bones of his ass.'

'But Klaus did give Jack the tip-off?' Latch asked her.

The woman shrugged. 'He could have, I guess.'

'Which means Jack must have worked a flanker,' Latch said.

'A double-cross?' Raejean asked.

Latch nodded. 'Jack must have sold the pictures on his own behalf and left Klaus out at the final reckoning; but then Jack would surely know it was Klaus putting the screws on him now.'

'And he doesn't know it's Klaus?'

'He hasn't got any idea who it is.'

'How do you know that?'

'He'd have told me if he'd known, surely. He asked me to come down here to protect Rachel and Marcia. If he'd known who I was supposed to be protecting them against, surely he would have told me.'

'Quod erat demonstrandum,' Rachel said with conviction. 'Klaus can't be behind the threat to me and Mother.'

'On the other hand,' Raejean said, 'if Klaus did recover the pictures, it would get him back into the fold with the baroness. She'd have to pay back the insurance money, but then she'd probably make twice that with the pictures at auction.'

'How do you know that?' Latch asked her. 'Do you know anything about the art market?'

'My father just happens to own one of the finest collections in America,' Raejean said. 'That's how I came to meet Klaus, at Parke Bernet in New York. I went there with my daddy, who was interested in a drawing by Albrecht Dürer—and guess who was selling it? Good old Klaus. Klaus was highly impressed by my daddy, as who wouldn't be with a guy who can buy a Dürer drawing out of his small change? I too was impressed, Klaus's aunt was a baroness, for God's sake. If I married Klaus, maybe I'd get to be a baroness

116

someday too, or at least a duchess or a princess or something. I didn't understand then that as she had no issue of her own, the title died with her and by the time I found that out it was too damn late and I'd married the bastard.'

'Where did he get the Dürer drawing from?' Latch asked.

'They had a collection.' Raejean began to pace the carpet as she spoke, the slit up the side of her robe exposing her long left leg to Latch as she was heading astern. 'The baroness's husband brought them back from the war. Loot. The Shauern-Oberhulzes lived moderately well simply by disposing of one or two pictures at auction every five years or so. By the time I came to Europe as Klaus's wife, they were down to the two pictures in question, one of which they thought might be a Goya, and the other an hitherto unknown Dosso Dossi. She sent them to the Ruijksmuseum for positive identification, and the clan's wildest dream came true. They'd hit the jackpot, because the big picture *was* a Goya, and the little one was a genuine old master.'

Latch lay back across the divan, against the uphol-stered bulkhead. 'Still,' he said, 'none of it makes any damn sense at all.'

'Not if you continue to insist that Klaus is behind this threat to me and Mother,' Rachel said.

'And I do, because he is. I saw him there with the men who were going to let that eel in with you, and that damn thing would have torn you to ribbons.'

Rachel stood with her back to him, remembering what she had seen when she looked down into the main chamber of the aquarium from the platform on top of the big tank—the water swirling about the floor and

117

a thick black thing glimpsed momentarily as it broke the surface.

'And you still believe Klaus over me,' Latch said to her.

Without turning, she said to him, 'Very soon I'm going to know who to believe and who not to, Sammy. Very soon now.'

'What does that mean?'

The girl said nothing; she remained standing with her back to him, in enigmatic silence.

'Tell her,' Latch said to Raejean. 'You're in on it, you bitch. If Klaus is in on it, you must be, so tell her the truth.'

'Assuming there is anything to be in on,' the woman said, 'why must I be in on it? You might not have noticed, but my so-called husband and I lead completely separate lives. The only times I ever see him are when he wants money. Then I give him money or he beats the hell out of me. Sometimes I give him money and he still beats the hell out of me; I'm getting to enjoy having the hell beaten out of me. I'm getting to be sick like that, you know? The other night at Cap d'Antibes I really enjoyed that, seeing him kick the shit out of you, Sammy Latch, and I think if I saw him do it again, I would probably enjoy it twice as much.'

The girl was looking at her almost with pity, and Raejean's plump, college-kid face was bitter as if she might cry at any moment.

'Why do you stay with him, then?' Latch asked her.

'I told you,' she said, balling her fists and spitting the words at him: '*I enjoy it!*'

Inside his blanket, Latch shivered. 'Does he belt you around as well?' he asked Rachel.

'He's a cruel man.' she admitted. 'But I'm beginning to believe that all men are like that.'

Raejean was back at the liquor cabinet recharging her glass. Latch said, 'Can I have another cigarette?'

Raejean lit one and handed it sideways to Rachel without looking at her.

'Don't let him get at you,' Rachel said to her. 'He's a pig.' Then she walked across and handed the lighted cigarette to Latch as if she were dropping the garbage down the disposal chute.

Accepting the cigarette, Latch said, 'You two make me throw up. A couple of noble, innocent maidens caught up in the machinations of evil men. You're either pretty damn evil yourselves, or you're pretty damn stupid.'

Raejean flashed him a glance of nickel-plated hatred.

Latch said to her, 'You saw the dapper little geezer I was with at the bar. Who is he, Raejean?'

'How the hell should I know? I never saw him before.'

Then Latch sat forward, looking from the woman to the girl and back again as he asked them: 'What does Sergeant Schuler's grave mean to you?'

'Sergeant who?' Rachel asked.

'Sergeant Schuler's grave,' he repeated.

Rachel looked blank. 'What should it mean?'

'It's something to do with where Jack has hidden the pictures,' Latch said.

'It means nothing to me,' Raejean said.

It apparently meant nothing to either of them. A whistling sound issued from a speaker in the forward bulkhead. It stopped, then a man's voice said: 'Cap Sicie coming up now, madame.'

Latch shut his eyes and tried to think; he got as far as

119

thinking that perhaps he had botched it and that perhaps Marcia and Rachel were now in deeper danger than before, because the deadline had been extended for that meeting in the aquarium, and the meeting had turned out to be a fiasco; but beyond that, his mind was full of the pain in his hand.

He needed the pain killed, desperately, and he needed time to think.

21

Dawn was breaking as the *Walkyrie* moved into the landing stage below the clinic at Cap Sicie. Rachel came ashore with Latch, and the boat turned around and took Raejean von Schanze back the way they had come. As the girl helped him up the long concrete stair from the landing stage to the garden on the cliff-top, Latch asked her:

'What's the project you mentioned, that you need the money for?'

'You'll know,' she said, 'in due course.'

'Is it what you were referring to when you said you would know who to believe?'

'Yes, it is.'

'Listen to me,' Latch said, an urgent note in his voice, 'the deadline they set for Jack expired three days ago. The end of the month they said they'd kill you. It was extended because of that appointment I had this morning in the aquarium. They're not going to extend it again. So you're living on borrowed time.'

'What do you suggest I do?'

They were halfway up the stair and Latch found that he had to stop for a spell. His head spinning, he leaned on the wooden rail.

'There's a chance,' he said, 'that as I recognised

Klaus, they will lay off. I'll cable Wallace and tell him about Klaus, so that if you or I or Marcia gets hit at least Wallace will be able to give Jack a lead on who did it, you see? They'll understand this, and that if they kill one of us, one of them might get killed in return, and it just might put them off, but it's far from certain so I'm going to get Marcia out of here and hide her up somewhere. And you've got to come with us.'

'Don't worry about me, Uncle Sammy. I'm getting out too, but not with you and Mother.'

'Not with Klaus,' he said, '*please*!'

'On my own,' she said.

'Where are you going, Rachel?'

'You'll know,' she said again, 'soon enough.'

On the cliff edge above, the silhouette of a woman stood against the paling sky. Her voice floated down on the light breeze off the sea: 'Sammy?'

'He's here,' Rachel called back, and Marcia came running down the steps to meet them.

They X-rayed the hand, renewed the plaster, and told him that wetting it had probably negated everything Professor Tollinger had done. Latch took the admonition unemotionally. Maybe he would lose a hand, maybe a life, and maybe even his own life. The fact that Marcia had stayed here all night waiting for him, making herself sick with worry over him, made the lives more important than the hand. So long as he had her, the loss of anything else was endurable.

When they wheeled him back to his room she was there with Rachel. Marcia helped the nurse put him to bed. Now that they had deadened the pain in his hand, exhaustion battered at him so that he had to force himself to remain conscious.

Rachel said, 'I'm going now.'

'For God's sake . .' but he could not stop her.

She glanced at her mother, then left them.

'You know,' Marcia said, mildly alarmed, 'I don't think she's got anything on under that bathrobe she's wearing.'

Poor old middle-aged bloody Marcia, Latch thought, inwardly shrivelling at the thought of telling her what her daughter had been doing in the fish-tank at l'Hirondelle.

'She's up to something,' he said. 'Get a cab and follow her, but discreetly. Just find out where she goes.'

He saw the woman nod.

'I'm going to sleep now,' he said, his eyes closing against his will, 'whether I want to or not; but as soon as I surface, we're getting out of here, with or without Rachel, we're getting out . . .'

If we're still alive when I surface, he thought, and then his mind slid over into oblivion.

He woke at about four in the afternoon, his hand throbbing like Christ. The sun glowed dimly through the dropped venetian blind. He got out of bed and staggered into the bathroom and swallowed several pills for the pain. Then he washed and shaved as best he could and returned to the bedroom and raised the blind. Blinking to ease his eyesight into the brightness of the day, he found that Marcia and Doreen and Freddie Norwood were sitting on the terrace with drinks on the table. Opening the window, he stood there naked to the waist in his pyjama trousers and said, 'Hi there.'

'How do you feel?' Marcia came towards him.

'Bloody rotten,' he said, watching Freddie Norwood dispense a long Scotch and ice and accepting it gratefully when Freddie handed it back to him.

He sat down at the table with them, the sun warming his back. 'How long have you been here?'

'About an hour,' Marcia said.

'We're having eel for supper,' Doreen grinned at him.

'No,' Latch demurred. 'It's too soon after the last one.'

'He was on the news broadcast at lunch-time,' Freddie said, 'your last eel, that is.'

'How is he?' Latch asked.

'He's fine, apparently,' Doreen said. 'They put him in another tank, and he appears to be just fine.'

'I'm relieved to hear it,' Latch said. 'The poor old bugger.' Then he said to Marcia, 'Did you follow Rachel this morning?'

The woman was sipping a Tom Collins. She nodded at his question, then said, 'She went back to the flat at La Ciotat, dressed, packed a bag, then took a taxi to Nice airport and got on a plane to London.'

Latch was smoking a cigarette. 'London?'

Marcia nodded, watching him through the lenses of her sunglasses.

'She's gone to see Jack,' Latch said.

'That's what I thought,' the woman said.

'That was the project she had in hand, that she needed the money for, to find out who to believe. She's going to blow the whistle on us to Jack.'

'Jack Carmody, you'll find, is a reasonable man,' Freddie Norwood said.

Latch looked at the old man in silence for a moment.

Then he said, 'Whittaker told me you had guaranteed Tollinger's fee. That was very kind of you.'

'Think nothing of it, old boy,' Norwood said, looking embarrassed.

'It wasn't necessary,' Latch said. 'My insurance covers this kind of thing. But it was still very kind of you.'

Lord Norwood said, 'Marcia has told us about this threat to her and Rachel. I s'pose you know that.'

Latch looked away from him, down at his drink. 'You had a right to know,' he said.

'Why don't you go to the police?' Freddie asked him.

'What could the police do? All they can offer is protective custody.'

'Do you have a better idea?'

Latch looked at Marcia. 'We've got to get out. Now, this evening.'

'Where are we going to go?' the woman asked him.

Doreen Norwood said, 'What about Roger's?'

'Yes,' Freddie said. 'Why not?'

Roger was the Norwoods' son-in-law who had a farm in northern Provence. He was not in residence at the moment and Freddie offered to telephone the housekeeper and tell her that Latch and Marcia were coming and ask her to let them in and look after them there. Latch had reservations; the place sounded too close to home, so to speak, but the idea of a farmhouse attracted him, an isolated place where any strangers hanging about would be immediately conspicuous.

'Yes,' he said at length, 'all right,' and looked at Marcia.

'I'm game,' she said.

He had a question or two he wanted to put to Marcia, as soon as they were alone.

125

22

They left just after dark, Latch driving Marcia's Alfa which he could manage because it was left-hand drive. He kept a fairly constant watch on the rear-view mirror in case they were followed, but as far as he could tell they were not. An hour after setting out they were high in the Alpes de Provence and it was raining heavily. Latch found the driving too difficult now, with one hand, so he pulled into the side and changed seats with Marcia. In the passenger seat he lit himself a cigarette while she looked ahead through the sweep of the wiper blade and notched first gear. When they were back on the road, Latch said to her:

'How did you come by that apartment in La Ciotat?'

'Some friend of Jack's arranged it. I don't know who it was.'

'Rachel told me it was Klaus.'

'Klaus?' She sounded puzzled.

'Did you know Klaus's aunt owned the pictures Jack stole?'

'What?'

'The Baroness von Oberhulz or whatever, who owned the pictures that Jack stole, is Klaus's aunt.'

'My God!'

'You didn't know?'

'Rachel told you this?'

'And Klaus was Jack's accomplice on the job. Klaus gave the tip-off that enabled Jack to do it.'

'Good God,' the woman said softly, plainly astonished. 'But how,' she went on, 'why . . . ? I mean how did Klaus and Jack get together to begin with? I understood it was somebody Jack knew during the war—and during the war, Klaus would have been a schoolboy . . .'

'That puzzles me, too,' Latch said. 'But that's the story Klaus has told Rachel. He is the baroness's nephew though; Raejean confirmed that.'

'But if Klaus was in it with Jack, it can't be Klaus who's threatening him now.'

'Not unless Jack had doubled-crossed him,' Latch said.

'Do you think that's what he's done?'

'No. Jack's not the double-crossing type; and if he had worked a flanker, he would have a pretty good idea of who exactly was screwing him now, don't you think?'

'Yes,' she said. 'Of course he would.'

'And I don't think he knows,' Latch said. 'I don't think he's got any idea who it is. Do you? I mean you've spoken to him, do you think he's trying to pull a fast one?'

'No,' she said. 'He hasn't got a clue who it is and it's tearing him apart to know who it is.'

'That's my conviction too,' Latch said. Then he said, 'Has he ever mentioned a thing called Sergeant Schuler's grave to you?'

She frowned, watching ahead through the windscreen and the rain the road like a black river flowing

127

through the beam of the headlights. 'Where did you hear that?' she asked.

'What does it mean, Marci?'

'It was years ago, just after I first met him,' she said. 'He told me about when he was shot down over France during the war. He parachuted into a field somewhere, I forget the name of the place, and some people there helped him, the Resistance. There was a First World War cemetery there, thousands of graves all the same, just marked with crosses. One of the graves was a dummy—the top of it was turfed over and looked exactly like all the others, but underneath was a sort of concrete bunker, and they hid Jack in it when the Germans came looking for him. He actually lived in this grave for two or three days, I think.'

Latch had sat up in his seat and was staring at her. 'For Christ's sake, girl,' he said, 'that's where the pictures are!'

'What? In the grave?'

'Where else? That bloke in the aquarium said: "It's Sergeant Schuler's grave, how do I locate Sergeant Schuler's grave?" That's what he said. They know about the cemetery, they just don't know which grave or how to find it. You've got to remember where this place is, Marcia.'

She drove in silence for a while, frowning in concentration. At length she shook her head. 'I can't,' she said. 'Anyway, Sammy, even if I could remember it, what good would it do? We'd know where the graveyard is, which is as much as your little man in the aquarium knows, and it obviously isn't enough. We still wouldn't be able to tell him how to locate the grave.'

'I've got to know where this place is,' Latch said.

She looked around at him; there had been a certain urgency in the tone of his voice, and she saw it again in his face, in his eyes, as he looked back at her in the thrown-back glow from the headlamps. 'Why have you got to know?' she asked him.

'So I can be there waiting for them, if Jack spills.'

'You mean if Rachel—or me—is killed.'

'It's the only lead I've got on them,' Latch said.

'What about Klaus?'

'There are two more besides Klaus. I've got to get all of them.'

'Well, I just can't remember, Sammy. I'm sorry.'

'Would you know the name if you heard it again?'

'I don't know. God, it was twenty years ago he told me about this place.'

'There can't be a hell of a lot of First World War graveyards around, can there? The Commonwealth War Graves Commission—that's the outfit, isn't it? They'd know where they all are, they'd have a list or something . . .'

'No,' Marcia said. 'It's not one of ours. It's one of theirs.'

'German? Of course—Sergeant Schuler . . .'

She nodded. 'The German ones aren't attended, you see. They're not maintained like the Allied ones are.'

Hell, Latch thought, picturing old Jack, hiding from the Germans in a German cemetery. 'Still,' he said, 'if there's a German one there, there would probably be an Allied one too, no? If the Allies got some of them, they almost certainly got some Allies. They're all up on the Somme, aren't they? Flanders fields and all that.'

Grim-faced, Marcia said, 'I really wouldn't know, Sammy. And quite frankly, I don't care.'

129

'What do you mean you don't care?'

She glanced into the rear-view mirror, then pulled the car into the side of the road and stopped. Then she turned in her seat to face him. 'If they kill me,' she said, 'I don't care whether you kill them or not. It isn't going to resurrect me. And I am not under any circumstances going to go charging off to the other end of France to look for a German graveyard right now, if that's what you have in mind.'

'And what about if they kill Rachel?'

'The same thing applies. Killing them isn't going to help her.'

For a moment, he scowled at her in silence. Then he said, 'That's a pretty callous attitude for a mother to adopt.'

'Sammy, don't you think Rachel has had enough warnings, pleas, and inducements? Don't you think I've shed enough tears for her and you've suffered enough pain for her already? And she still elects to treat us like filth. Don't you think we've done everything we possibly could for Rachel. And you've done more . . .' she looked at his left hand, '. . . you've sacrificed practically your life for her, to no avail. Do you really think it's worth pursuing the pantomime over Rachel?'

He lit a cigarette.

'What I said the other morning in the clinic,' she went on, 'I meant that, Sammy. From now on there is just you and me. Practically all my adult life I've been torn between you and that girl; while she needed me, I stayed with her. Now she rejects me, for whatever reason, because she thinks I'm a whore, because I *am* a whore, because I'm back-dooring Jack, whatever is her reason, it lets me out. She won't accept me, or my advice or guidance, she's declared me redundant. So from now on, I'm out of her way and she's out of mine. And there is just you and me.'

He inhaled deeply on the cigarette. Her attitude was believable and understandable to him; but the other thing still frightened him, the threat to her life.

As if seeing this fear in him, she said, 'If I've only got a couple of days before they come to get me, I want to spend them the way I wish to Christ I could have spent my whole life. In bed with you. But until they come, I want to forget them. I want there to be just you and me on that farm in Provence, and nothing else existing in the universe. Rachel is Jack's problem now, Sammy. If he has any feeling at all for his daughter, he will tell these people where he hid his bloody pictures, and that will be the end of it. But from now on, there is just you and me, and the killers and the pictures and Jack and Rachel and all the rest of it just do not exist for me.'

His cigarette was finished and he opened the car window a fraction and flicked the butt out into the rain.

The farmhouse at Ste Estephe les Arbres was a large, barn-shaped place of dark grey stone under a slate roof. From their bedroom window, in the late morning sun, Latch could see across a deep valley the grape harvest in progress among the vines that covered the farther hillside. The laden, horse-drawn wagons moved so slowly in the leaden heat they seemed to be motionless, stationary between the rows of dusty green vines. Down in the valley a stream bickered along to join the brimming Rhône somewhere to the south and west, and then to spread out over the endless flat miles of the

Camargue. Behind him in bed, Marcia was eating a late breakfast.

In front of the house stood two enormous plane trees with an iron pump over a well between them permanently enveloped in their voluminous shade. In the afternoon, Latch and Marcia walked into the village, about three miles away, and had a few drinks at the inn there, and watched the locals playing boule in the dust by the roadside. It was pleasant sitting there at a wooden table in the shade, with a beer, and the woman beside him, brushing at flies under the wide, floppy brim of her white lace hat, watching the hard, leathery men keen-eyed as the big steel balls sailed through the air, dropped in the powdery dust, rolled and clicked against other steel balls in the sunlight; but still Latch could not relax.

'Listen,' he said to her, 'didn't it ever occur to you that this grave is where he'd probably put the pictures?'

'God, you just can't forget it for five minutes, can you?'

'Didn't it occur to you? Didn't you think of the grave?'

She nodded. 'Once. The first night you arrived in La Ciotat and you asked me if I had any idea where he might have hidden the pictures, it occurred to me then. I hesitated in answering you, and I could see you didn't believe me when I said no. But that's why I hesitated, because I'd thought of Sergeant what's-his-name's grave; but I dismissed it.'

'Why?'

A short man in a black beret and a gaily coloured shirt was about to throw his boule.

'Oil paintings, Sammy, are perishable. If you put them in a damp old hole in the ground, they will deterior-

132

ate. Jack expects to be out of circulation for the next fifteen or twenty years—what sort of condition would those pictures be in after fifteen or twenty years underground? They'd be ruined.'

She was looking at him across the table, but he was sitting side-on to her, one arm resting on the table top, watching the style of the short man swinging his boule preparatory to launch.

Then he said, 'Not if they were in a damp-proof, air-tight container.'

'Even so, it can't be the best hiding place in the world, either,' Marcia argued. 'There must be other people around who know about it, besides Jack. What guarantee would he have that the pictures would still be there after he came out, after twenty years inside? I personally believe it's the last place on earth he'd have put them.'

The short man swung his arm and the steel ball traced a shimmering parabola above the roadside, and dumped heavily in the dust.

Latch nodded, in appreciation of both the short man's swing and Marcia's argument. 'But he might have put them there for somebody else to pick up,' Latch said, still on the subject of the pictures and Sergeant Schuler's grave. 'You still can't remember the name of this place?'

The woman sipped her drink, a long, green one comprising among other things a good deal of crème de menthe and ice, then shook her head negatively.

'Can't or won't?' Latch said.

She sighed heavily. 'Honestly, Sammy, if I thought for a minute it would do us any good at all to know, I would try. But it would simply be wasting time, and

133

we've wasted so much time already, I just don't want us to waste any more.'

'Not even if it saves Rachel's life?'

'How? How is it going to save Rachel's life? What else can we do to save Rachel's life? Is there anything we haven't tried already?'

That leg of the boule game was over and the players were laughing and joking, performing autopsies on their play, lighting the thick brown cigarettes they smoked as they picked up their boules.

'We could find the pictures and hand them over,' Latch said, 'to whomever it is that wants them.'

For a moment, she looked at him in silence, faintly surprised at what he had suggested. Then she said, 'Do you mean that?'

He nodded.

'What about Jack? What about your dear friend Jack, and your loyalties, and all the rest of it?'

'I'm beginning to feel the same way as you do about Jack,' he said, reflectively. 'I was willing to go along with him while there was time to do something about it; but now the deadline's expired, if he won't hand those pictures over to save his wife and kid, I think somebody ought to do it for him.'

'You've changed your tune, haven't you?'

'What do you mean?' he looked at her.

'Last night you wanted to know where this place was so that you could go there and wait for these people to come, and kill them, or let them kill you. Today, you want to hand them the pictures.'

'Is that why you wouldn't tell me where it is?'

'Sammy,' she said softly, 'it may sound terrible, and cruel, and wicked—but suddenly, you are more important to me than Rachel.'

'Is that why you won't tell me where this place is, Marci?'

'I don't know where it is, Sammy, And even if I did, what good would it do? You said the men in the aquarium knew about the grave, they just couldn't locate it in the cemetery is what you said. Suppose we found the cemetery—if they can't locate the grave, how are you going to?'

She had a point of course. Latch banged his plaster cast on the wooden table top out of sheer frustration. 'I just want to be doing something,' he said. 'I can't just sit around here waiting for them to come for you, or to hit the girl.'

For the first time she got some idea of how he felt and what was bugging him. He was scared, not for himself so much, but for her. In his hip pocket, she knew, he was carrying her little Beretta; he carried it with him everywhere now.

'All right,' she said.

He looked around at her. 'All right what?'

'Tomorrow,' she said, 'we'll go over to Valence. There'll be a public library there; they should have a list of First World War graveyards and their locations. If I see the name again, it might come to me.'

He almost, but not quite, smiled with relief at her. Then he said, 'Promise?'

Sadly, she nodded, not looking at him.

'Marcia,' he said, 'I agree that the grave is an unlikely place for him to have hidden the pictures; but it must have some bearing on the problem for these geezers in the aquarium to have been so damn interested in it, do you see?'

Again, not very interestedly, she nodded.

'Maybe the pictures aren't in it,' he went on, 'but

135

there must be something in it. A clue as to where they are, or something, you see?'

The sun was going down. The boule game seemed to have ended.

'You finished?' she asked, looking at his drink.

23

In the morning, as Marcia had promised, they drove to Valence and went to the municipal library there. The librarian, a helpful, fat woman in her thirties, recommended them to the appropriate volume of an encyclopaedia, the section headed War Graves. This listed the locations of several dozen First World War graveyards, all printed in four-point type, any length of which was exceedingly difficult to read, but Marcia sat down at a table with it and embarked on the task. Latch watched her for a while, then started pacing, then lit a cigarette and was told to put it out by the fat librarian, then found a file of magazines and tried to read one of them. At length he put the magazines down, stood up and started pacing again.

He looked across at Marcia and found her looking up at him and shaking her head slowly. There seemed no point in arguing any more; she was genuinely distressed at having failed him. He went to her and stood behind the chair she was sitting on and put his good hand on her shoulder.

'No?' he said.

'It could be any of them,' she said. 'I thought if I saw it again it would come back, but ...'

'Was it a one-word name or a compound?'

'I can't even remember that much,' she said. 'Sammy, it was twenty years ago . . .'

'All right,' he said. 'Let's go and have lunch.'

Driving back to the farm that evening, Latch thought, looking at Marcia: Another day gone, and she's still alive.

But what about this time tomorrow?

Each evening, Freddie Norwood phoned just to check that they were both still alive and to report on any developments at his end. Apart from the B.B.C. news from London, which Latch usually picked up on the car radio, Freddie was his only contact with the world at large, and by now he was coming to look forward to the old boy's calls. The gist of that evening's chat, as it had been of the previous evening's, was that there was nothing doing, either at Bandol or at Ste Estephe les Arbres. Then, before retiring, Latch inspected the locks on every door and window in the house to ensure that the place was as impregnable as he could make it. But it was still with a certain amount of relief that he awoke in the morning and found Marcia still breathing in the bed beside him.

How long could it last? he wondered. For ever? Had the threateners really been bluffing after all? Had that little bastard been bluffing in the aquarium as the grille was going up and the eel was feeling his way towards Rachel in the other half of the tank? If he was bluffing, he was a damn good bluffer, and anybody who could bluff like that didn't need pictures, even a couple of million quid's worth of pictures; he could have made a bloody bomb playing poker.

Their fourth day at the farm, they picnicked in some woods a few miles to the north. The sun, unhampered as ever, shone magnificently, and Marcia took her clothes off, shielded from the road by some big trees and a high, green mound, and lay down on a towel in the long green grass naked. Her skin shone like a dully iridescent alloy with milk-white patches that Latch sat trying to avoid looking at her, conscious of her nakedness, but trying not to let it get him randy. He failed spectacularly.

Then he lay beside her in the sun and said, 'Are you too old to have a baby?'

The question seemed to surprise her and she turned over, propped on one elbow, looking down at him. Then she laughed. 'For God's sake, what sort of a question is that?'

He shrugged. He didn't know what sort of a question it was. 'Are you?'

'No,' she said.

He grinned at her.

'Why?' she asked.

Again, he just shrugged, and she lay over him and put her hands one either side of his face and studied his face gently and with tenderness. Then she put her mouth on his and they kissed. He had made love to her and was spent, so they kissed now gently but with deep emotion rather than the urgency of passion, her naked body against his, sweating together in the heat of the sun but brushed by a soft breeze that moved through the grass around them.

'Do you want me to have one?' she asked him.

He was toying with her hair, twisting coils of it round his fingers. 'Maybe,' he said.

'Do you want a son or a daughter, Sammy?' she asked him softly. 'To play the piano for you?'

He looked at the tip of her nose, barely an inch

139

from his own. 'That would be pretty good, I think.'

'I want to have your baby, Sammy.'

He grinned. 'You'll probably find you're going to whether you want to or not.'

She laughed, lying back on the grass with her arms spread and her eyes closed, laughing freely, with happiness, an unpolluted laugh.

He looked at his watch. 'Time for the news,' he said.

'Damn the news,' she said.

He put his undershorts and jeans on and went back up to where they had left the car in the shade of the big trees by the side of the road. Sitting on the front seat, half in and out of the car, he turned the radio on. It was a good radio, and with only a little background crackle, the B.B.C. man's voice came to him immediately, halfway through a sentence:

'. . . *escaped from Parkhurst Prison on the Isle of Wight.*

'*A Home Office spokesman said this morning that Carmody had escaped . . .'*

Latch yelled down the slope: 'Marcia!'

'*He had obviously had expert outside assistance, the spokesman said.*

'*Police threw a cordon around the Isle of Wight, sealing all airports, rail-ferry stations, and yacht marinas, but the cordon has since been relaxed as it has become apparent that Carmody is no longer on the island . . .'*

Marcia had thrown her dress on hurriedly and was clambering up the slope towards the car. 'What is it?' she called.

'*An ex-Battle of Britain fighter pilot, Carmody is thought to have escaped by air either to the Continent*

140

or Southern Ireland. The Eire constabulary and Interpol have been alerted.

'Jack Carmody, husband of the singer Marcia Carmody, was sentenced to twenty years' imprisonment at the Old Bailey in June after . . .'

Bare-footed, the woman arrived by the car just in time to catch the last paragraph. Wide-eyed, she almost shouted at Latch: 'What's he *done*? What's happened?'

'He's out. Over the wall.'

She stared at Latch for a moment in a kind of stupefied silence, then whispered: 'Oh my God . . .'

'Expert assistance,' Latch said. 'That would have been Franco Porcia. Porcia sprung him.'

'Why?'

'For money, of course. If you can pay his price, Porcia can get anybody out of pokey.'

And that job would have cost a bomb, he thought; Parkhurst was maximum security—it would have cost probably twenty thou.

'I mean why did he escape just now, at this particular moment, just after Rachel's been to see him, Sammy, to tell him about us. Don't you see?'

'Don't talk rubbish, Marci. Do you think he cracked out just to come and punch me on the nose for pussyfooting with you? That's rubbish. It's the other business, the threateners; that's how that bastard Porcia operates, playing both ends against the middle, collecting from the threateners that are putting Jack through the wringer then collecting from Jack when old Jack decides it's time to do something about it.'

The woman stood by the side of the road watching Latch steadily. The sunlight swamping the world behind her silhouetted her naked body through the thin cotton

141

dress and her bare feet in the dust had the texture of suède leather. 'What's he going to do about it then?' she asked him.

He shrugged. 'Get your things,' he said. 'We better get back to the house.'

24

Inside the house the phone was ringing. Marcia put the car under one of the big plane trees and as she and Latch were walking towards the front door, the phone was still ringing. He wondered why the housekeeper didn't answer it. The door was closed but not locked. He opened the door, went through the lobby, across the living-room, and picked up the phone.

'Latch! At last I've got you!' It was Freddie Norwood.

'What is it, Freddie?'

'I've been trying to get you since about 10 a.m. Now listen. My chauffeur didn't appear for breakfast this morning. I thought he might be sleeping off a bender, so I let him lie a while. When he hadn't surfaced by ten o'clock, I went up to his quarters. He was in there on the floor, bound and gagged. Three men had worked him over sometime during the night, trying to get him to tell them where you and Marcia are. He doesn't know, of course, but he does know my son-in-law has the house at Ste Estephe Les Arbres, and he fears that *in extremis* he might have mentioned this to these men.'

A cold claw seemed to grip Latch's innards.

'How long ago?'

'He's not sure of the time, but it was before dawn.

143

They've had plenty of time to get to you, so I shouldn't even bother to pack a bag. I should just jump in your car and go straight to the police, Sammy.'

'Did you ring earlier?' Latch asked.

'Twice. Both times I got the housekeeper. She said you were out picnicking somewhere and that she'd tell you to call me as soon as you got in. I rang now because you were taking so damn long to call me I thought she might have forgotten.'

'Okay, Freddie, thanks.' Freddie started saying something else, but Latch said, 'Be seeing you,' and put the phone down. Something was up. The housekeeper should have been here. Even before he turned around, he knew that there was a man in the room behind him.

He was short and neat and wearing a dark, lightweight suit, a pearl-coloured, intricately self-patterned shirt, and kipper tie. He smiled with considerable charm and said to Latch: 'The circumstances of our first encounter, Monsieur Latch, were at best uncomfortable, at worst downright ludicrous. I am happy to meet you again in saner conditions.'

The first encounter to which he referred had taken place in the main chamber of the aquarium aboard l'Hirondelle. He was the dapper little man.

Almost instinctively Latch reached for the gun in his hip pocket.

'Oh no, not that damn thing again,' the little man sounded pained. 'Before you break out the ordnance, Sammy, take a look out of the window here.'

Latch walked across to the front window and looked out between the slats of the venetian blind. Marcia was standing by the well in the shade of the big trees, and there was a man there with her leaning on the pump above the well. He was fat, wearing a Stetson

144

hat, sunglasses, and a loud, Hawaiian-type shirt outside his trousers. From between his fat lips, a fat cigar protruded, and in the crook of his left arm rested a 12-bore shot-gun.

'You will observe,' the little man said from behind Latch, 'that we've brought a piece of our own this time, and that it's of rather heavier calibre than yours. One barrel, at that range, would cut Mrs. Carmody in half; and that's what we're going to do, unless you do exactly as you are told.'

Latch turned. The little man was standing there with his hand out and Latch took the Beretta from his pocket and handed it over, butt first. 'What have you done with the housekeeper?' he asked.

'I telephoned her from the village and told her I was a doctor and to get over to her brother's place, which is about twelve kilometres from here, immediately, as there had been an accident. Off she dutifully scuttled, dutifully panicking like mad.'

'Who the hell are you?' Latch said.

'My name is Claude Garnier. I am an old friend of Jack Carmody. Has he never mentioned me?'

'No,' Latch said. 'Do you know Jack's out?'

'Is he? I didn't know; but I expected he would be, any day now. He's a rich man, why should he linger in prison?'

'I think he'll be wanting to talk to you, Mr. Garnier.'

'I doubt it,' the little man smiled. 'Why should he? He has his money, his wife and daughter are unscathed, and now that we know how to locate Sergeant Schuler's grave, we have the pictures. So everything has turned out all right in the end.'

'You know how to locate the grave?'

Garnier nodded. 'A message reached me from Jack last night, telling me how to do it.'

So Jack had cracked. 'Then why are you here?' Latch asked. 'Jack's told you what you want to know—you can't have any further interest in his wife. You don't need to kill her now, or threaten her any more.'

'That isn't strictly true, I'm afraid. Jack has told me how to find the grave; but possibly he has lied—given me a bum steer as you might say, to buy time for himself. And against that extremely unlikely event, I want to be insured. Marcia must come with us. So, I fear, must you.'

Latch looked back through the slats of the blind. 'Come with you where?' he asked.

'To a place called Dimeaux, in northern France.'

Marcia was still standing out there, under the plane tree, glaring at the fat man with the gun. That was the fat man from the aquarium, and his cigar; here in the room was the dapper little man; there was just one more unaccounted for.

'Where's von Schanze?' Latch asked.

Garnier grinned. 'It was most astute of you to have recognised him that night.' He was calm and quite collected, and although he was unmistakably French, his English was excellent.

'Where is he?'

'He's gone on ahead to Dimeaux—with his estimable wife.'

'I knew that bitch was in it.'

'Sammy, my friend, I'm sure you are just as anxious as I am to get this affair ended. We have a long drive in front of us, so do you think we could be on our way?'

'Do you mind if we pack our bags first?'

'You will pack the bags. Come on, I'll watch you.'

Latch led the way upstairs. This was it, he was thinking; now, after several days of worrying and wondering, how and when it was going to happen, how and when they were going to come, now he knew.

In the bedroom, Garnier stood by while Latch tossed his and Marcia's things into their bags.

'You said you're an old friend of Jack's,' Latch said.

'I met him in Dimeaux during the war. It is my home town, you see, and during the war I was a member of the Resistance there. Jack was an R.A.F. pilot on the run. It was my task to take him to Sergeant Schuler's grave and hide him in it.'

'Well, if you showed Jack where the grave is, how come you are now screwing *him* into telling *you* where it is?'

The little man chuckled, standing easily with his hands in his trousers pockets. 'That's a good question,' he admitted. Then he said, 'You see, all this started when Klaus von Schanze decided to steal his aunt's pictures. He had a ready market for them—our friend outside there with the shot-gun. He is paying a million dollars in cash for those two pictures. All Klaus then needed was a little bit of technical knowhow—somebody actually to do the job for him. He came to me. I am an art dealer, I have a small gallery in Paris— and a reputation for being able to supply—difficult items, you understand?'

Latch continued packing. He understood.

Garnier was over by the window, looking down through the net curtain. 'I thought of Jack for the job for several reasons. Firstly, the pictures were going to be stolen in transit from the Ruijksmuseum to Sotheby's in London, and as Klaus was privy to the details of the transfer, he was automatically going to be suspected, so the further away from Klaus the better for actually doing the job. That meant it had to be done at the other end, England. I'd kept in touch with Jack over the years since the war—the odd reunion, you know, in Paris and in London. I thought he was ideal for it. So I contacted him, and with information supplied by Klaus, Jack planned it and executed it perfectly. After doing the job, he flew the pictures, as we'd arranged, back to Dimeaux and deposited them in Sergeant Schuler's grave for collection by me. Then he flew back to England and was, unfortunately for him, arrested.'

'I can't close these bags with one hand,' Latch said.

Garnier nodded sympathetically. He took the Beretta from his jacket pocket and said, 'Well, stand over there by the wall and I'll close them for you.'

Latch retreated to the wall.

As he closed the bags, Marcia's three pieces and Latch's camel-hide grip, the little man went on:

'These German war graveyards, you know, are not tended as the Commonwealth and American ones are. This one at Dimeaux would be a complete wilderness, except for the fact that the local farmers graze their sheep on it. It is just a field of several hectares, with some eight to ten thousand graves each marked solely by a little black wooden cross. Each cross is in every way identical to every other cross, except of course for the name inscribed on it. You follow?'

Latch nodded.

'When I got to the graveyard and tried to locate Sergeant Schuler's grave,' Garnier went on, 'I found that Jack had switched the crosses around, he had switched maybe thirty or forty crosses around, which meant that the grave marked by the little black cross with the name of Sergeant Schuler on it was no longer the dummy that contained the pictures. And there was just no way, short of digging up the whole damn field, of finding that dummy grave unless you knew the name on the cross that now marked it. You see? That's why I had to screw Jack. How many of these can you carry with your one hand?'

Latch looked at the luggage on the bed. 'Two,' he said.

'I'll bring the other two. You go ahead.'

Struggling downstairs with one bag in his hand and another under his arm, Latch said, 'Why should Jack do that? Switch the crosses around like that?'

From behind him, Garnier said, 'There is only one logical reason.' Then after a pause, he said, 'Think about it.'

The only logical reason, that Latch could think of anyway, was that Jack had worked the proverbial flanker; he had already flogged the pictures and left his partners in the crime out of the final reckoning. Which meant that the grave at Dimeaux was empty and that Garnier's insurance—Marcia—was going to be turned in for whatever it was worth.

25

The afternoon now was advancing, and the sun was cooling off; in the shade of the great plane trees by the well it was almost dusk. The little man left Latch and Marcia and their luggage there in the custody of the fat man with the shot-gun, while he went off down the road a way to bring up the transport. They had left their car down there so as not to advertise the presence of strangers at the house.

Under the brim of his Stetson the fat man wore dark glasses. He removed his cigar from his teeth, however, to nod and say, 'Howdy,' to Latch.

Latch returned the nod. Then he said to Marcia, 'The name of that place you were trying to think of . . .'

'Yes?' Her voice was strained, over-controlled, and when she looked at him her eyes were wide and intense.

'Dimeaux.'

'Oh?' She just managed to sound interested. It meant nothing to her. 'Who was on the phone?'

'Freddie.' Latch looked at the fat man. 'Warning me that our friends were on their way.'

The fat man grinned. 'Left it a bit late, didn't he?' His accent was a nice, soft, cultured, southern drawl.

There was a familiar ring to it, and something familiar about his fat, soft, baby mouth.

Latch said, 'We met once in the aquarium, right?'

The fat man nodded, smiling, moving the shot-gun from the crook of his left arm to grip it by the stock in his right hand. 'You really put on one hell of a show that night, Sammy. I didn't get a tremendous kick out of it at the time, mind you, but in retrospect it was surely one hell of a show.'

'You're Raejean von Schanze's father,' Latch said.

'How'd you guess?'

Latch shrugged. 'She told me about you. You're a collector who can buy Dürer drawings with the small change out of his sidepocket. And you're prepared to pay Klaus a million dollars for those two pictures. And you're the spitting image of Raejean.'

'Abe Decker,' the fat man said. 'And you're right. Raejean is my daughter.'

Latch said nothing.

'What are you going to do with us?' Marcia asked the fat man, Abe Decker.

'I'm hoping, Mrs. Carmody, I won't have to do anything with you.'

'You mean you're hoping the pictures are in Sergeant Schuler's grave at Dimeaux?' Latch said.

'That's what I'm hoping, Sammy.'

'You're a mad optimist, Decker. If Jack hadn't double-crossed you, why would he go to the trouble of switching the crosses around?'

'Anybody could have switched the crosses around. Kids playing pranks, sheep could have knocked them over and some do-gooder put them back in the wrong places . . .'

'As I said,' Latch repeated, 'you're a mad optimist.'

151

A big black Lincoln Continental turned in from the road and sighed to a stop beside them. Claude Garnier was at its helm. Latch and Garnier put the luggage in the trunk. Latch was directed into the rear seat and Decker, with the shot-gun, got in beside him. Marcia sat in front, with Garnier, who was driving. As the car moved back up onto the road, Latch put a cigarette between his lips and pressed the lighter in the armrest of the seat.

'Mr. Garnier,' Latch said.

'Yes, my friend?' Garnier spoke over his shoulder, without looking around.

'You said, back in the house, Jack has his money now—what exactly did you mean by that?'

'From the pictures, his money from the pictures,' Garnier said. 'Jack has his cut already.'

'How can he have his cut,' Latch looked at Decker, 'if the buyer hasn't paid off yet?'

Garnier chuckled. Then he said, 'Maybe you had better explain that one, Abe.'

Shifting his cigar from one end of his mouth to the other, Decker said, 'No, Claude. You know more about the snake on the grave than I do.'

'Oh yes,' Garnier nodded. Then he said softly, 'The snake on the grave.'

'What is the snake on the grave?' Marcia asked, still tense, like a caged bird.

'It's an expression we used during the war,' Garnier said. 'It means the grave is booby-trapped. It's a warning: Don't attempt to open it, or you'll die . . .'

'And the grave is booby-trapped now?' Latch asked.

Taking his cigar between thumb and fingers, Decker nodded. 'The snake's on it,' he said softly.

'It was a precaution we had to take,' Garnier said.

'Only one person at a time knew the combination for opening the grave safely. Because there were a number of things we kept in that hole in the ground that we could not have allowed the Germans to find—lists of names, codes, passwords, and so on. You understand? So there were about fifty pounds of gelignite attached to the underside of the cover over the grave, and you had to know exactly the correct method of removing that cover or you got spread very thinly all over the Pas de Calais.'

The fat man beside Latch examined his cigar butt and came to the conclusion that it was exhausted. He pressed the button to lower his window a fraction and jettisoned the butt, then raised the window again.

'After Jack put the pictures in the grave,' Decker said, 'he reset the snake. A new charge, a new method of removing the cover without detonating it. This was part of the deal. Claude agreed he would do this. The directions for opening the grave, Jack put in an envelope which he lodged with a bank in Zürich with the instruction that the envelope be handed over to whoever came to that bank and deposited five hundred thousand dollars to Jack Carmody's account.'

Latch nodded. 'Smart,' he said softly.

'Damn smart,' Decker agreed. 'It guaranteed Jack his cut whatever happened; but then the bastard has to go and put frills on it. I handed over five hundred gees to that bank in Zürich and they handed me the envelope. Then Claude and me and Klaus went back to Dimeaux—and found that the goddam crosses had been switched around and we couldn't find the goddam grave.' The fat man took a deep, wheezing breath, controlling his emotion, which was pretty profound at this stage. 'So right about then,' he said, 'I started getting a little worried.'

Marcia was turned around in the front passenger seat to look over the backrest at Decker. They were heading north and a road-sign they passed said LYON 87 km.

'Even then,' Garnier said, 'we thought perhaps there had been a mistake, or a misunderstanding, or some kind of human error. So I went to London. Jack was in custody then but he had not stood trial, so his lawyer had pretty free access to him. I went to see the lawyer and told him it was most urgent he explain to his client that the crosses had been inexplicably switched around and we could not locate Sergeant Schuler's grave, so could he please help us, as his money had already been paid into the bank in Zürich. Back came the lawyer with Jack's polite reply—my regrets, Claude, he said, but it will cost you another half a million.'

Latch was half tempted to laugh, but he resisted it; he noticed too that the humorous side of it had not escaped Garnier.

Abe Decker, on the other hand, found nothing at all amusing about it, possibly because it was his money that was being bandied about with such reckless abandon.

'That's when I decided to put the rollers over the bastard,' Decker said, softly, raising his gaze to take in Marcia. 'Jack was inside and untouchable; but his wife and kid weren't.'

Latch stubbed out his cigarette and raised his left hand in its plaster-cast above shoulder level. It was beginning to throb slightly and he had found that raising it like this eased it.

154

'So Jack must have known that it was you putting the pressure on him,' he said to Decker.

Decker nodded and took a cigar pouch out of the pocket of his shirt. 'I got in touch with a friend in New York,' he said, shaking a cigar up in the pouch, 'and he recommended me to a guy called Porcia in London, and Porcia delivered my message to Jack who by this time was in Parkhurst.' He bit the end off his cigar and set about lighting the thing.

'What I mean is,' Latch said, 'did Jack know who the threat came from, apart from Porcia?'

'Well, I wouldn't say he knew for certain,' the fat man said while drawing vigorously on the cigar, 'you see, Sam, when you smuggle threats into jailhouses, you're wiser not to sign your name on them, you know? But I would say that Jack was in a position to have made one hell of an educated guess, wouldn't you?'

'He should have been,' Latch agreed, 'but he didn't, because he had no idea where that threat came from.'

'Then I would say that Jack was either pretty stupid or he just wasn't opening up his heart to you, Sambo.'

Garnier said: 'He wouldn't have told you, Sammy, that he was in the act of double-crossing his partners, would he? In fact we're reliably informed that all he asked you to do was get Marcia and Rachel out of France, right? He didn't ask you to take up arms against Abe and Klaus and me on his behalf—you just did that for the hell of it, or the sport, or for other reasons known only to you.'

'Who's your reliable informant?' Latch asked, grimly. 'Or need I ask?'

'Boy, Sammy,' Decker shook his head, laughing silently, 'If I had friends like little Rachel, I would quit making friends.'

155

The fat man's cigar smoke was fogging up the inside of the car and in self-defence Latch lowered his window a little and lit himself another cigarette. Marcia had turned right around and was looking straight at Latch. Then she turned to Decker and said: 'Was it Rachel who set Sammy up to get his hand smashed?'

Garnier answered her. 'In fairness, Marcia, I don't think Rachel imagined that Klaus would go as far as he did on that occasion. She just thought they were going to kick Sammy around a little, she did not envisage the business of the hand.'

Marcia's lips were set hard and tight. 'The bitch,' she whispered.

'I just don't believe,' Latch said, 'that Jack Carmody would try such a stupid, clumsy, two-timing trick.'

'The facts are before you, my friend,' Decker said. 'The deal was costing me a million dollars—a half to Jack, a quarter each to Garnier and Klaus von Schanze. Before the deal had gone through, Jack says double my cut. Now where I hail from, that's a double-cross.'

They rode in silence for a while, Latch smoking his cigarette, Decker sucking his cigar, Marcia, with her head down, wrapped in private thought, Garnier watching the highway over the top of the steering wheel, the needle of the speedo, which was calibrated in m.p.h., hovering around the hundred mark as the big car surged ahead in effortless silence.

After a while a rather alarming thought occurred to Latch. 'The directions for opening the grave,' he said, 'if Jack's double-crossed you, then it follows that the pictures aren't in the grave anyway. So he's probably given you the wrong directions.'

Decker removed the cigar from his mouth and frowned and pursed his lips, assuming an attitude of profound concentration preparatory to a launch into oratory. 'It's like this, Sam,' he explained, like an old pro showing a new boy the ropes, 'there is just a remote possibility—as you say—that Jack Carmody does not give a continental horse's ass whether his wife and daughter get hit or not, and that he has worked a real lulu of a double-cross on me, in which event he has already disposed of the pictures, and the grave is, as you say, empty. In which case, I agree with you, it's a distinct possibility that he has given us the wrong combination for opening it, in the hope that we'll blow ourselves to smithereens.'

'That's why we're bringing you along, Sammy,' Garnier said. 'You're performing the opening ceremony for us.'

26

They stopped once, in a town somewhere, at a delica-
tessen store and Garnier went in and came back loaded
with food and a couple of flasks of wine. They ate and
drank in the car on the move. Latch and Marcia had to
take their turns driving while Garnier or Decker got
some sleep in the back seat; but all the time one of
them was sleeping, the other was constantly alert,
armed with the shot-gun and the little automatic. They
passed through Paris in the early hours of the morning,
Marcia driving, because at that hour it was quicker to
go through the city than to skirt it, and emerged on
the other side onto the Autoroute du Nord for the final
leg of the long run north. They arrived in Dimeaux
towards noon, and there, parked in the forecourt of
an inn, was Klaus von Schanze's black Porsche.

The inn was the Auberge St. Auguste, and it
appeared to be the only hotel in the town, which lay
athwart a *route secondaire*. On the other side of the
road was a service station with two Antar petrol pumps
in front of it, then a terrace of yellow, steep-roofed cot-
tages, then a bar-tabac, and the whole place was silent
and deserted under deep-bellied, battleship-coloured
clouds.

Garnier parked the Lincoln beside the Porsche and

opened his door. 'Wait here,' he said, getting out and slamming the door. He went up the front steps and into the inn. In the back seat of the Lincoln, with Decker and the shot-gun beside him and Marcia in the front passenger seat ahead of him, Latch sat smoking a cigarette. Marcia was turned around in the seat, staring at him. At length she said, 'If I had ever dreamed that Carmody could have let you in for this, I'd have murdered him in his sleep.'

'Forget it,' Latch said, barely concealing his shakes.

Garnier emerged from the inn followed by Klaus and Raejean von Schanze. Despite the fact that he had had only three or four hours' sleep in the back seat of the moving car, Garnier was still highly mobile and alert. Klaus came down the steps of the inn and grinned through the window of the Lincoln at Latch. Garnier got back in behind the wheel. He turned in the seat and said to Latch:

'We're going straight over to the cemetery now and have a look at the grave. You won't be able to open it until after dark, but it will help if you have a look at it in daylight first.'

'Get stuffed,' Latch said, with feeling.

The graveyard was less than a kilometre from the inn, and Klaus and Raejean in the Porsche followed the rest of the party in the Lincoln. When they got there, Latch appreciated the difficulty one would have had in attempting to single out one of the graves from the rest. Rows of small, black, wooden Teutonic crosses stood in precise longitudinal, latitudinal, and diagonal alignment on a flat green field that must have been five acres in area. There were thousands, all exactly similar, constituting collectively an enormous and grisly monument to the beast in man.

In a place like this, Latch realised then, somewhere in North Africa, his own father lay.

The men alighted, Decker holding the shot-gun on Latch. Garnier gave the Beretta to Raejean who got into the Lincoln to guard Marcia and the other four headed out into the vast and silent necropolis, in search of Sergeant Schuler's grave. The instructions Garnier had received from Carmody said the grave lay in the 79th line from the south-east corner and was the 244th cross from the east end of the line. The name on it turned out to be that of one Private Helmut Geitz.

It was not difficult to locate and once located they found that superficially it was no different from any other of the graves there.

In the distance, among the crosses, some sheep were grazing under a low and leaden sky. The awesome silence of the place prompted Claude Garnier to rhetoric:

'It's hard to believe,' he said, 'but less than fifty years ago this place was a sea of blood and mud, pocked and scarred by shell-craters and trenches, scoured and sterilised by mustard gas, torn by barbed wire and bullets, ringing with the screams of dying men. Death pollutes the place; have you noticed—the sheep over there never seem to bleat, as if they fear to desecrate the silence. The elements, through some inconceivable cosmic imperative, are dulled and muted here, so no wind stirs and no bird sings, as if in awe of the enormity of the things that were done here. Sammy, my friend, I hope everything goes all right for you tonight.'

Latch stood at the foot of the dummy grave, marked by Helmut Geitz's cross. 'I understand Jack Carmody actually lived down there for a few days—in that hole in the ground.'

Garnier nodded. 'He spent several nights down there, shoulder-to-shoulder with the dead. Just Jack and several bottles of cognac. If that doesn't account for his periodic deviations from the behavioural norm —what in hell's name could?'

Abe Decker said, 'Seen enough?'

'I think so,' Garnier said.

'Let's get back to that hotel then,' Decker said. 'I need a shower and a shave. Among other things.'

As they walked back down the long lines of crosses towards the cars, Latch said to Garnier: 'How am I supposed to go about opening it, then?'

'After dinner,' Garnier said, 'we'll bring you out here and relocate the grave, remove the turf and topsoil for you. It's a not too strenuous dig, just about ten or twenty centimetres of earth.'

The women were still sitting in the Lincoln, Marcia in front, Raejean behind her with the automatic. The men stood around the bonnet of the big car and Garnier took a folded sheet of paper from inside his jacket and handed it to Latch.

'Suppose I refuse to do it?' Latch said, looking at the piece of paper.

Abe Decker, his Stetson pushed back on his bald head, leaning with his backside against the car, spoke through the end of the cigar that was clamped between his teeth. 'You're at liberty to reject the commission, of course, Sammy.' Then his eyes went hooded and stony, like an alligator's eyes. 'But then a number of nasty things might start happening to your lady friend in the car there.'

Marcia was sitting in the car watching them through the windscreen.

161

Latch put the piece of paper down on the bonnet of the car and started unfolding it.

'I should read it very carefully, Mr. Latch,' Klaus von Schanze cautioned.

Using only his right hand, Latch was having difficulty opening the paper out, and Klaus took it from him and unfolded it and spread it on the bonnet for him. It was neatly typewritten on one side only.

'This cost you half a million dollars?' Latch asked Decker.

The fat man nodded and let go a billow of cigar smoke into the still afternoon air.

'Before you read it, Sammy,' Garnier said, 'you should understand this. The casing containing the explosive is attached to the underside of the cover of the hole, see? The cover itself is nothing, just a sheet of asbestos. The casing is fixed to the cover by six screws, two long, two short, and two intermediate. The detonating mechanism is a trigger held in the cocked position by a plastic thong. Above the thong is a small reservoir full of nitric acid. If the mechanism is tilted by so much as a minute of a degree out of the horizontal, the acid will spill from the reservoir and burn through the thong, releasing the trigger to detonate the explosive. You cannot raise the cover without first detaching the explosive from its underside, and that is done by withdrawing the six screws in strict sequence. The piece of paper in front of you gives you the sequence.'

On the paper were six numbered points, representing the screws:

1. 2.
4. 3.
5. 6.

Under the numbered points were the instructions:

'The diagram shows how the screws are numbered standing at the foot of the grave, facing the cross. The screws are coupled as follows: 1 and 3, short traverse; 4 and 6, intermediate traverse; 5 and 2, long traverse; each couple must be removed in that order. The removal of the short traverse screws lowers the casing five centimetres to the point at which it is supported by the intermediate traverse, but still attached to the cover; the removal of the intermediate traverse lowers the casing another five centimetres to a point at which it is held by the long traverse, but still attached to the cover; the removal of the long traverse detaches the casing from the cover—the snake on the grave has then been defanged, and the cover can be raised.'

At the foot of the page was a final direction, which Latch had to read three times before fully grasping its significance:

'It is essential that the two screws in each couple are withdrawn exactly, turn-for-turn, simultaneously.'

Latch handed the paper to Garnier. 'What does that last bit mean?'

Garnier, for some reason, smiled at the query, and without bothering to look at the paper, as if he had in fact been waiting for Latch to ask that question, he said:

'I should have thought it would have been obvious. Each pair of screws, as you are unscrewing them and until they are completely withdrawn from their holes, are the sole support of the device underneath. If one screw should get by so much as a single turn ahead of its mate, the device will tilt—and detonate. So each pair of screws must be loosened, turn-for-turn, simultaneously.'

163

Klaus was leaning with one arm on the hood of the car, his chin in his hand. 'Surely you can manage that, Mr. Latch?' he asked.

'How,' Latch asked, raising his plaster-encased left hand, 'do I undo two screws simultaneously with one hand?'

The three men examined Latch's plaster cast as if it was a phenomenon completely new to them; but on Klaus's sharply-chiselled, deeply-tanned face, the smile froze over like the tundra under the first icy blast of winter.

'I think, *mes amis*,' Claude Garnier said at length, 'that Mr. Latch has a point.'

'God damn!' Abe Decker said, still looking at Latch's left hand. 'He can't do it. There is no way he can do it.'

At this point, unable to contain their curiosity any longer, the two women emerged from the car and Raejean said:

'What in hell are you characters discussing out here, anyway?'

'Get back in the car,' Klaus ordered. 'Both of you.'

The women hesitated, Raejean bristling and getting ready to rebel; but Abe Decker said to her, 'Go on, honey, get back inside with Mrs. Carmody. We'll be with you directly.'

Unhappily the women got back into the car.

'Latch can't do it,' Garnier said. 'It's physically impossible for him to do it.'

'Which rather obvious flaw in our logic having been pointed out,' Decker said. 'we are left with a problem. If Latch can't do it, who can?'

Garnier raised his eyebrows and looked from

164

Decker to von Schanze, and back again. 'It'll have to be one of us,' he said.

Abe started to look nervous and began puffing more vigorously on his cigar. 'I reckon,' he said.

'What do you reckon?' Klaus asked him.

'I reckon it'll have to be one of us.'

'Why will it?' Klaus was scowling unhappily.

'Because, my friend,' Garnier said to him quietly, 'you maimed Latch.'

'But why one of us?' Klaus persisted. 'There is still Marcia Carmody. Why should one of us risk it? If Carmody has fixed the thing to blow up, why should he not blow up one of his own—his wife for instance?'

Klaus seemed pleased with this suggestion, expecting it to be accepted as a good idea. When it was greeted with an awkward silence, he began to looked puzzled.

'What's wrong with that?' he asked, looking from Decker to the little Frenchman.

Garnier looked down at the stones on the gravel roadside. 'What kind of a man are you?' he asked von Schanze. 'You're no kind of a man. You're not even a dog.'

'To force a woman to do a job you don't have the intestine to do,' Decker said, watching the German, 'takes a pretty sick kind of a dog.'

Suddenly and decisively, Garnier said, 'You'll do it, von Schanze.'

Latch had a funny feeling that this was what they had been working up to, that Garnier at least, and possibly Decker too, had known all along that it was Klaus who was going to be tackling the snake on the grave.

'What?' Klaus blinked at Garnier.

'Besides,' Decker said, 'you make the woman do it,

165

even if she's got the right combination, she'll be shaking so god damn much she'll probably blow herself sky high anyway.'

'It will take a young, strong, and steady hand,' Garnier said. 'You, Klaus, are the youngest and strongest, if not the steadiest, among us.'

'And as it was you who eliminated Latch from the challenge round anyway,' Decker went on, 'you would seem to be most deserving of the honour.'

Klaus was all of a sudden looking embarrassed.

'Look, Klaus,' Decker said comfortingly, adopting his avuncular attitude, 'Carmody couldn't believe that if the thing blew up, all of us would be crazy enough to be close enough to go up with it. He must have known that two, or at least one, of us would survive. He knew also what was going to happen to his wife and kid if he persisted in playing silly-buggers, right? Now would the guy deliberately jeopardise his wife and daughter like that? Hell no, Klaus; look, I'm a family man, and I'm a tough bastard, but no family man is that tough, boy, believe me. The thing has to be okay, you follow? This combination we have here just *has* to be correct.'

'Then why don't you open the grave?' Klaus asked him, reasonably enough.

'Because the consensus of opinion holds that you are better qualified than he is,' Garnier said to von Schanze. 'And because you've been outvoted.'

27

Klaus had taken a room at the Auberge St. Auguste for the sake of convenience—they did not intend spending a night there; but they used the room in turn for bathing and changing. Latch was supervised at his ablutions by Garnier, and Marcia at hers by Raejean. Afterwards, shaved, showered, and freshly clad, they regrouped in the bar downstairs for aperitifs before dinner. The place was well patronised, mostly by itinerant salesmen and Belgians and Germans passing through on their annual treks south and west. Marcia was hugely relieved to hear that Latch no longer had the prospect of opening the grave hanging over him, and she appreciated the irony of it when she heard why he could not do it and who was doing it in his stead. For the moment it did not seem to be bothering Klaus too much—he was drinking beer and chatting unconcernedly with Garnier and Abe Decker and Raejean. But during dinner he did not touch the wine and he did not eat very much, and at the end of the meal he excused himself and went to the toilet.

As soon as Klaus had gone, Abe Decker said to Garnier: 'He's peeing himself with fright. It's dark enough, so I'm going to drive him out there now and get it over. You and him will get your payoffs when we get back with the goods, okay?'

'Abe,' Garnier said, 'listen, Abe. If he gets an attack of the shakes while he's taking the screws out, he just might blow himself to kingdom come whether the combination is right or not, so I would stand well clear while he's doing the job if I were you.'

'I intend to, old friend,' Decker said with feeling.

When Klaus returned, Decker stood up and said to him, 'Ready then?'

Von Schanze nodded. His eyes were bright and there was a fierce look in them.

'Good luck,' Latch said, and smiled reassuringly at him, and Klaus turned on his heel and went, followed by Decker.

The dining room was emptying. Only a few lonely commercial travellers lingered at their tables, working on reports or reading newspapers or paperbacks with their coffee.

'I think we need another bottle of wine,' Garnier said, and signalled the waiter accordingly.

Then suddenly Marcia sat erect, staring across Latch's shoulder towards the far side of the room. 'Sammy!' she said.

Latch turned in his chair and at first saw nothing extraordinary, four or five men finishing their meals at different tables. Then he noticed, at one table on the far side of the big room, a man and a girl. The girl had her back to the room, but the man was facing in Latch's direction, a big man with close-cropped black hair, wearing horn-rimmed spectacles and a dark, pinstripe suit. He was just sitting there with his back to the wall, staring towards Latch. As Latch looked at him, the big man suddenly grinned, and the girl at the table

168

with him turned in her chair and showed her face. It was Rachel.

Slowly, Latch stood up. The big man did likewise and came around his table and moved the girl's chair out for her as she too rose. The big man came across the room, negotiating a path between abandoned tables and empty chairs, followed by Rachel, and he stood in front of Latch and bowed stiffly from the waist. 'Ernst-Werner Schmieder,' he said, in a passable German accent, 'of München. And I have a passport to prove it.'

'Jack!' Marcia gasped.

'Hush,' Jack Carmody admonished her. 'Herr Schmieder, if you don't mind.'

Rachel stood just behind her father. She was wearing a very neat suède minidress with shoes made of the same suède, and her black hair was tied up at the back of her head to leave her long neck and shoulders bare. She looked beautiful, as always, and she stepped up to Latch and held his good hand in both of hers.

'Sammy,' she said, and he saw that there were tears in her eyes. 'I can't ask you to forget what I've done to you—but I would do anything, anything, anything, if you could ever forgive me . . .'

He put his arm round her. 'Forget it, honey,' he said.

Jack Carmody was looking at Latch as the girl put her head down on Latch's shoulder.

Carmody said, 'Sammy, one of the reasons I came over here was to meet the bastard who did that to your hand. Where is he?'

'He's otherwise engaged at the moment,' Latch said.

'That was him that went out a few moments ago with the fat fella?'

169

Latch nodded. 'Sit down, hey?'

'Where have they gone?'

'Come and sit down, Jack,' Garnier said. 'And we'll tell you all about it.'

Carmody fixed the dapper little man with a cold and menacing gaze. 'As for you, you two-timing son of a whore . . .'

Garnier raised his eyebrows and looked unjustly accused and innocent as a dew-kissed daffodil.

Carmody sat down. Rachel sat between Marcia and Latch holding her head low and wiping tears from her face. Marcia put her arm around the girl, and Rachel broke down completely, sobbing aloud and whispering, 'I'm sorry, Mummy, I'm so sorry . . .' and her mother held her as if she was a little girl again, distressed at her little girl's heartache, trying to comfort her.

Jack Carmody was looking across the table at Raejean von Schanze. 'Who's she?' he asked rudely of no one in particular.

Garnier explained who she was while Raejean sat in arch and injured silence, radiating contempt for Carmody and his boorishness.

When he knew who she was, Carmody nodded, then looked down at the table top. 'Sammy. I'm sorry as hell about the hand.'

'Have a drink,' Latch said to him.

'How did you get here?' Marcia asked him, still with her arm around Rachel.

'Porcia sprung you?' Latch asked him.

Big Jack nodded. 'The standard contract; I had it arranged with Porcia before I even went in. Ten thousand to get me over the wall, another ten thousand for a new name and passage to a foreign port.' He stroked his short, dyed hair and tapped the plain glass lenses of his horn rims. 'A real pro is old Porcia. It's the little touches you can tell us by and there are very few of us left, Sammy.'

'And Rachel came along with you?'

'Why not? Listen, Sammy, until Rachel came to see me in Parkhurst I had no idea who was putting the screws on me. I honestly didn't. Then she told me what happened to you in that aquarium, three men, a fat one with a cigar, a dapper little guy, and another one, and they knew about Sergeant Schuler's grave. It took me a minute to figure it out—then it clicked. One of those bastards was trying to make it look as if I was working a double-cross. And the only reason why he should want to do that was that he himself was working a double-cross. Right, Claude?'

Garnier said nothing. He just smiled at Carmody and took a sip of wine.

'It had to be Claude,' Carmody went on, 'because he was the only one of them who knew how to locate the grave. I *knew* he knew how to locate the grave, he could find that grave in the dark, whether the crosses were switched around or not. And he was stalling and making it look as if I was the double-crosser, while he was working a fast one on his partners. Soon as I worked that out, I told Rachel to go straight up to London and see Franco Porcia and give him the necessary references for finding the grave for immediate onward transmission to his principals—who just had to be Claude Garnier's partners in this deal. Right?' To Garnier, he said, 'I take it they're out there trying to open the grave now?'

The little Frenchman nodded.

'How did you work it, Claude?'

Latch had been thinking. 'I'll tell you how he worked

171

it,' he said. 'I've just worked out how he worked it.'

Garnier smiled at him.

Latch said, 'After Jack did the job and deposited the pictures in the grave, you came up here to Dimeaux and switched the crosses around. Then you took Abe Decker to Zürich and he handed over half a million dollars in exchange for the combination for opening the grave. You memorised that combination. Then you came back to Dimeaux, with Abe and Klaus, and tried to open up the grave with Sergeant Schuler's name on it. It turned out to be a real grave. So Jack Carmody must have switched the crosses around, so you couldn't locate the one with the snake on it. So then you told Abe and Klaus you would have to go to London to see Jack; but you didn't go to London; while Abe and Klaus *thought* you were in London, you were out there in the graveyard—you had the combination, and that was all you needed. You opened the grave, took the pictures out, and flogged them. Then you went back to Decker and von Schanze and reported that Jack was demanding another half a million for telling you how to locate the grave.'

The wine bottle was empty and Garnier was signalling for more. 'This is a very interesting theory, Sammy,' he agreed solemnly.

'Then when old Abe Decker decided to start prodding me,' Carmody said, watching the Frenchman, 'you knew exactly where to find Marcia and Rachel, in La Ciotat, because you fixed the apartment there for them. I asked you to do that before I even did the job.'

Rachel had recovered sufficiently now to be following the conversation. 'Klaus said he arranged the apartment for us,' she said.

'Klaus was just trying to make a big feller of himself, honey,' Raejean said. 'As usual.'

'But because Claude Garnier knew where we were,' Marcia said, 'Klaus was able to go down there and get his hooks into Rachel.'

The waiter had brought more wine and Garnier was sampling its bouquet. He decided it was acceptable and shooed the waiter off. They were the only people left in the dining-room now and were proving a source of considerable annoyance to the waiter.

Then Carmody leaned forward on the table and said, 'How much did you get for the pictures, Claude?'

'My dear Jack,' Garnier sighed, pouring wine all round, 'my dear Sammy, suppose I said you were right? Suppose I admitted to this terrible thing you accuse me of. What then? It's all over now and nobody has been hurt—except Sammy, with his hand, and I had nothing to do with that. Nobody has even been in danger—except Sammy again, and that was danger in which he deliberately placed himself. So what?'

'What about Rachel? You were going to let that damn eel have her.'

'No.' The little man shook his silvery head. 'Never. I was bluffing. Sammy called my bluff; immediately he called me, I stopped the partition rising, no? I could have left the switch down and she'd have been sucked out through the hole in the glass, torn to pieces by the glass if not by the eel; but I switched it off, no? It was all bluff, *mes amis*, and it's all over now. As I say, the only person hurt is Sammy, and I had no part in that, I can assure you.'

Marcia said, 'Surely you were putting Sammy in danger by forcing him to open that grave tonight?'

'I knew he couldn't do it, madame. I knew he couldn't possibly do it with one hand; but I had to let

173

him point it out to the others. I could not give them even the slightest hint that I was on Sammy's side, could I?'

'Which brings us back to the grave,' Latch said, 'and what's in it. As you've already disposed of the pictures, I take it there's nothing in it.'

'You are wrong, monsieur,' Garnier said. 'There is about twenty kilos of gelignite in it.'

'And you used Jack's combination to open it, and when you replaced the cover you changed the combination of the screws,' Latch said. 'So tonight, Klaus is going to try to open it using Jack's original combination, which now is wrong.'

Garnier sat back in his chair, took a mouthful of wine, and dabbed delicately at his lips with his table napkin. 'Which will solve the problem of Klaus,' he said calmly, 'for all time.'

At that moment the earth moved, as if buffeted by a mighty wind, and everybody froze, breathless, for perhaps half a second, until the buffeting subsided. It was immediately followed by a distant, dull crunching sound, like a great rock crashing into the street outside, and, from nearer at hand, the tinkle of breaking glass. The lights that hung from the ceiling were swaying.

'Don't be sorry about my hand, Jack,' Latch said softly. 'It's just saved my life.'

174

28

'Who bought it?' Jack Carmody asked, looking at Garnier. 'The young one?'

'I expect so,' Garnier nodded.

'You two-timing bastard,' Carmody said.

Garnier just sat there looking helpless and morose. Then Raejean asked, 'Does that mean that I'm a widow?'

'I think, *mon tresor*,' Garnier said to her, 'yes. I think that Klaus has made a balls of it.'

For some moments, the woman looked preoccupied, thinking about what had happened, and perhaps even regretting it a little. But she did not regret it long.

'Well, that's that,' she said, as if washing her hands of the whole business.

'What are you going to do about Abe?' Latch asked Garnier.

'Why should I have to do anything about Abe?'

'He might have twenty or thirty million stashed away,' Latch said, 'but he's still not going to be terribly pleased to discover that he's spent five hundred thousand on nothing.'

'He might have lost five hundred thousand,' Garnier said, and looked around at Raejean, 'but he has gained a son-in-law; and this time, a moderately rich one.'

Raejean burst out laughing. It was a release of great emotional pressure, a nearly hysterical laugh, and tears were coming from her eyes as she lay her head down on Garnier's shoulder and he put his arm round her and kissed her hair; she continued laughing and crying simultaneously, saying to Garnier, lovingly, adoringly:

'You little old bastard!'

Watching them in mild wonder Latch said softly, 'You worked it this way, right from the beginning—the pair of you, just to get rid of Klaus.'

'Not just to get rid of Klaus, Sammy,' Garnier explained. 'That was only one of our objectives. I also made some money out of it.'

'You really are a two-timing little snake-eyed bastard, Garnier,' Carmody said, almost in admiration.

'Everybody seems to call you that, Mr. Garnier,' Rachel said. 'Are you really a bastard?'

The little man gave her his Gallic shrug and his *ca-ne-fait-rien* smile. 'If I am, mademoiselle,' he said, 'I'm a rich bastard.'

'And the *real* snake on the grave . . .' Latch said.

'Is me, Sammy,' Garnier agreed.

'How much did you get for the pictures?' Big Jack asked him.

'About the same as you.'

'You have to say that, even though you got four times as much as me.'

'No,' Garnier smiled, shaking his head. 'I got about twice your cut, Jack; but half of it I am going to have to pay back to Abe Decker, who had to deposit that amount with a bank in Zürich in the name of some non-existent Boche called Ernst-Werner Schmieder.'

Carmody laughed. He laughed until he realised that nobody else was laughing, and then he stopped and

176

looked at Marcia. The woman was staring silently at the man who, for eighteen years, had been her husband.

'Don't worry, me darling,' he said to her, softly, almost sadly. 'I'm not going to prove an embarrassment to you, now or ever again.'

'What are you going to do, Jack?' she asked him.

'Going down to Bilbao. I'm catching a boat there for Rio, and I might buy myself a night-club over there.'

'If you do,' Latch said, 'don't call it the Sundowner.'

The big man grinned, then looked at Marcia, and Latch could see in his eyes that he wanted more than anything else on earth to take her with him to Rio; but he just said, 'She's all yours, Sammy. I think she always has been.'

'If you knew you could get out of jail,' Marcia said accusingly, 'Why did you send Sammy down to La Ciotat to do your dirty work for you?'

'What could I have done for you? If I'd gone over the wall the cops would have been following you around La Ciotat like a pack of rats after a cheese-wagon. They'd be here now if they knew you were here. An escaper on the run, they watch his wife and family like hawks. I couldn't have got near you, Marcia.'

The woman looked down. Rachel reached over and took hold of her mother's hand.

Carmody turned to Latch. 'Anyway,' he said, 'I can't hang around here too long. Is everything under control now, Sammy?'

'I reckon,' Latch said.

'Then I'm going to push off.' Carmody stood up and walked around the table and put his hand on Marcia's shoulder. 'See Lee Wallace in London,' he said to her.

'I've made some financial provision for you and Rachel.'

She nodded stiffly, holding the girl's hand, holding her own emotion down, not looking up at him. 'Thanks a million,' she said.

'And get old Sam to bring you down to Rio some day, huh?'

This time she just nodded.

Then he stood behind Rachel, holding her in the chair so that she could not stand up and face him. 'Goodbye, sweetheart,' he said.

Tears were streaming from the girl's eyes.

'And trust your mother,' he said to her. 'And Sammy. He's a better friend than either of us deserves.' Then he just slapped Latch lightly on the shoulder and said, 'See you,' and turned quickly and walked out.

For a while they just sat in silence, except for Rachel, who was hunched over with her face buried in her hands and sobbing bitterly. By contrast, Marcia's face was stone cold. A chapter in her life had ended and she was hanging in the empty zone between that ending and the beginning of something new. Latch reached for his wine and clumsily knocked the glass over. The wine stained the white linen table cloth and Claude Garnier reached over, righted the glass, refilled it for Latch, and handed it to him.

'Thanks,' Latch said to him, raising the glass.

'To Jack Carmody,' Garnier said, solemnly, raising his.

As they drank the toast, Raejean was looking towards the entrance to the dining-room. 'Here comes Daddy,' she said.

29

Abe Decker looked as if he had tangled with a combine harvester. He had lost his Stetson and all the buttons off his shirt-front, and all the stiffening in his hitherto immaculate suit seemed to have evaporated, leaving him clad in damp sacking. Latch went to him and helped him across the dining-room to a chair at their table.

'I was half a mile away,' Abe said, dazed, 'and it knocked me flat on my goddam back.'

'What about Klaus?' Raejean asked him, anxiously.

'There isn't enough left of Klaus to fill a cavity in a jack-rabbit's toenail,' the fat man said.

'At least it was quick for him,' Garnier said, stroking the bereaved widow's hand.

Then old Abe's face became thunderous and full of hate. 'That bastard Carmody!' he said with passion.

'Why do you say that, Abe?' Garnier asked him. 'How do you know it wasn't Klaus's own fault—that he was trembling so much with fright that he made a complete balls of it.'

'It's okay for you to get philosophical, buddy, but I'm down half a million bucks,' Abe said angrily.

'Not really,' Garnier said, soothingly, taking a slip of paper from inside his jacket and handing it to Abe.

Decker looked at the paper, then, frowning deeply, up at the dapper little man. 'Your cheque?' he said incredulously. 'For half a million dollars?'

'It will take seven days to clear,' Garnier said. 'But it will be honoured.'

Slowly the light dawned for Abe Decker. Then he roared at Garnier: 'It was you! *You* worked the double-cross!'

'I didn't say that, Abe. I didn't say that. What makes you think I can't write a cheque for half a million dollars?'

Then Raejean said, 'Papa, if you must know, it was I who double-crossed you, me, your ever-loving, blue-eyed little girl. I did it to get rid of that son of a bitch I was married to, and because I love Claude and I'm going to marry him.'

That was the second shock-wave to hit Abe Decker that evening, and like the first, it knocked the wind out of him. He just sat there leaning forward on the table with his mouth hanging open, staring at his daughter, not understanding, confused and beaten.

Latch stood up and put his hand on Abe's sagging shoulder. 'Let me be the first to congratulate you, Mr. Decker,' Latch said, looking at Raejean. 'With a son-in-law like Claude, who needs a Goya and an old master?'

Raejean and Garnier laughed; but old Abe, though he tried, couldn't raise one, and in fact ended up lowering his head onto his forearms on the table top and giving way to uncontrollable tears of sheer misery.

The Mistral was blowing, lashing through the trees and shrubs in the Norwoods' garden and flecking the long, dark sweep of the Mediterranean beyond with white.

Latch was sitting on the terrace with Lord Norwood, drinking Lord Norwood's fine whisky, watching the wind.

'How's the hand?' the old man asked him.

'I don't feel it any more,' Latch said. 'I suppose I'm getting used to it.'

A long white cruise liner was passing the point, rising and rolling in the swell with occasionally a big coamer hitting her and breaking and showering spray the length of her. The happy holidaymakers on her would be going to Butlins next year, Latch thought.

'John Whittaker came over a few nights ago,' Freddie Norwood said. 'Wanted to hear you play. Doreen put on a few of your records for him.'

'I suppose they gave him a pain in the arse,' Latch said, watching the liner heading for Marseilles.

'No, strangely enough, he's borrowed them to tape them.'

'The bastard,' Latch said. 'That's royalties I lose.'

'Gave me a pain though,' Freddie said.

'I'm sorry about that,' Latch said, taking a drink, listening to the music Freddie was listening to now, 'L'après Midi d'un Faun', coming from the speakers of the Norwoods' high-class hi-fi setup. 'I'm really sorry about that, Freddie, because now I'm going to give you another one.'

Freddie raised his eyebrows.

'The pictures you had hanging in the den the last time I was here,' Latch said.

The old man nodded and put his glass down on the table. 'You noticed them then,' he said.

'Not at first. Oh, I noticed them, but they just didn't register at first.' Latch looked back to the sea, where the big white ship was still at odds with the Mistral, and

181

Latch and Lord Norwood were sitting here watching it and listening to the delicate silences of 'L'après Midi', also at odds with the heaving wind, and drinking good whisky and talking about stolen pictures. The afternoon of Lord Norwood's come-uppance, Latch thought. 'I started wondering,' he said, 'after you'd been so good to me over the hand; calling in Tollinger and guaranteeing his fee and treating me as if I was your long-lost prodigal son. Marcia said it was because you were just good people, and I don't doubt that, I believe you are good people, but even good people aren't that good to a stranger.'

'Poor devils out there,' Freddie said, watching the cruise liner. 'Some fine dinners being tossed around out there I shouldn't wonder.'

'I remembered those pictures in your den when Raejean von Schanze told me about the pictures that Jack Carmody stole,' Latch went on, while the old man nodded his head in time with the rhythm of the music. 'A Goya and an old master, a Dosso Dossi. They were hanging on the wall in your den the first night I came here, with Rachel and Marcia. Right?'

Freddie was pouring himself another drink. He held the decanter up to Latch and Latch nodded. 'Right,' Freddie said, recharging the other man's glass, 'of course you're right. Damn foolhardy thing to do, I admit, but I'd only got them in their frames that day and I was so damn proud of them, and you and Marcia and Rachel did turn up unexpectedly that night. I didn't think you'd noticed them.'

'If I had,' Latch said, looking at his left hand, 'it might have saved me this.'

'I realised that. That's why I guaranteed Tollinger's money for you.'

182

'Well, you can do more than guarantee it,' Latch said. 'You can damn well pay it.'

'And then we're quits?'

'Quits,' Latch nodded.

'Agreed. Damn decent of you, Latch.'

Latch added a little water to his Scotch. 'You bought them off Claude Garnier, of course,' he said.

'That's right.'

'How much?'

The old man looked troubled. 'You don't want to know that, do you?'

'Yes. I do. How much?'

'Five hundred thousand sterling. In small denomination notes.'

Latch nodded. Claude had made a profit of about three-quarters of a million dollars. Tax free.

'What are you going to do with them, now you've got them?' he asked, meaning the pictures.

Freddie shrugged. 'Keep 'em a few years. Come to an arrangement with the insurance company. Then flog 'em. Probably make a million or two on them.'

'Money makes money, hey?'

'Damn difficult to do anything without it, old boy. Damn difficult.'

'You imagine.'

'Want to see them?'

'Yes,' Latch said. 'I'd like to.'

'Let's kill the bottle first, hey?'

'Fair enough.'

'Then we'll go down and have a look at them.'

There were about four fingers left in the decanter. On the tape deck, 'L'après Midi d'un Faun' ran out and the mighty opening bars of the Bach Toccata and Fugue swelled from the speakers.

183

'Schweitzer,' Freddie said. 'Did you ever play the organ?'

'Once,' Latch said. 'At school. The chapel organ. I got six on the arse for playing Handel with a boogie bass. It put me off the organ.'

'Assuming you can't play the piano again,' Freddie said, 'what are you going to do? Have you thought about it?'

'I might buy a place down here somewhere, and lie in the sun for a while.'

'Good idea, buying a place down here, sound investment. But I can't endorse lying in the sun. Bloody unhealthy.'

'Marcia and I are going to try writing some songs.'

'Good. Good thing. As long as you don't brood. You've suffered a great loss, son. But don't brood on it.'

'I think,' Latch said, picking up the decanter, 'that maybe I've found a bit more than I've lost. Ready?'

'Fill her up,' Lord Norwood said.